# HERE IS
# A GAME
# WE COULD
# PLAY

# HERE IS A GAME WE COULD PLAY

*a novel*

## JENNY BITNER

ACRE

CINCINNATI 2021

Acre Books is made possible by the support of the Robert and Adele Schiff Foundation and the Department of English at the University of Cincinnati.

ISBN-13 (pbk) 978-1-946724-40-3
ISBN-13 (e-book) 978-1-946724-41-0

Designed by Barbara Neely Bourgoyne
Cover art: iStockPhoto.com/Vizerskaya

The press is based at the University of Cincinnati, Department of English and Comparative Literature, McMicken Hall, Room 248, PO Box 210069, Cincinnati, OH, 45221–0069.

Acre Books books may be purchased at a discount for educational use. For information please email business@acre-books.com.

*To my mother, Carlyn Leicht Bitner,*
*who probably would not have approved of this book*
*but loved me always nonetheless.*

℈

# HERE IS
# A GAME
# WE COULD
# PLAY

## POISON DIARY

Women poison more than men. Women poison because we are told what we feel isn't real, what we see doesn't exist, what we trust is a lie.

We are poisoned, so we poison. Part of our job description is feeding men, and so we feed them.

# DEAR POTENTIAL LOVER,

I think about you all of the time. You are not really a certain shape or form or sex, but more of an idea. If you like to play games, maybe we could be lovers. Here is a game we could play.

*game one*

# PILLOWS

There is something I would like you to do for me. I have needs to be touched in certain specific, yet distant, manners. In this game, you apply pressure to my body without thinking about my body. I am lying in my bed, on my back, and you line up pillows around me. The pillows should be very tight against my sides, front, and head. You press on the pillows so it feels like I can't move.

Your arms are over my ears so I can't hear the neighbors mowing their lawns. I can feel your body, but only through the pillows. You hold me with a steady pressure I cannot escape. Essentially my choice is taken away from me, but the pressure is so comforting I don't care. I release my choice. It feels delicious for a moment not to have to be choosing and choosing.

Sometimes I don't know if people want to be touched and opened up or if they want to be alone. At the coffee shop near my work, I overheard two women talking. "I don't go in his sore place. He doesn't go in my sore place," one said. It seems like a good idea, but then who does go into the sore place, and will it ever become less sore? These are questions I'm working on.

*game two*

# LISTEN

Come closer. I have a story to tell you, even though I don't know who you are. I only know that you are exceptionally sensitive like the tentacles of a sea anemone and wise like a new baby who looks like he's lived his past life as a lama. You want to hear everything about me. You are patient. You are the perfect lover, or since nothing is perfect, the perfect lover for me.

I live in a country reconstructed from burnt-out memories, consisting of cakelike suburbs, of icing and dreams and no one to talk to who lives within walking distance. There is the ARCO station and the 7-Eleven and the dream lover on *The Bold and The Beautiful*. In other words, I live in small-town America in the last decade of the twentieth century.

I have always been odd. That is what some people say, and that is what I think. In a small town it's a matter of fitting in or not fitting in, and it's pretty clear early on who stands where. I never thought I was saying anything odd, but when I used "perhaps" instead of "maybe," the other children looked at me out of the corners of their eyes. Certain differences in thought set me apart and didn't allow me to become close to others.

When I first arose—impractical, scared—into the gray of this town, nobody much took notice. And that's how it's been ever since. There have been boys I've slept with here and there, the inevitable push of all that physical stuff, but not much to count on my list of life's achievements. I knew that virginity had gone from being sought after to being a liability, so I dispensed with it as soon as I could without breaking anything important.

I should explain some personal things about myself, give you a history of sorts. I'll tell you deeply secret things—the kinds of things I might reveal after sex. But we haven't had sex, so it is better, less motivated by a desire for you to see me a certain way. That is one thing I want—to be painfully honest. I won't lie or omit details just so you will love me.

The town where I was born, Riverton, population 14,347 and shrinking, is along the Susquehanna River in Pennsylvania. It was an old mill town and then became a steel town and now is sort of a ghost town, with large industrial monsters that just sit there, hulking metal monuments to the glory of fifty years ago, larger than you think anything needs to be, and with a once concrete purpose that is now entirely obsolete. Factories where very important things were made—things that were going to change the world for the better—now sit empty. Oh, people still live here, not like the real ghost towns in the West that only have dust and cacti blowing through them, but the energy has been drained away, and many of the people have the hollow look of having lost things: money, jobs, husbands, purpose. Maybe places like this aren't so much ghost towns but zombie towns. Everyone is still walking around, but are they awake? My parents were both born here, and my father worked at the steel mill until he didn't anymore, until he was gone.

When I was a child, my mother always asked me, "Where's your common sense?" as if it were a genetic problem and I had been born without this trait. She worked as a secretary down at the meat-packing plant, where they pumped the pink-gray ham full of water, and men flirted with her by calling her a good-looking woman. Old Mr. Harvey occasionally patted her rump when she bent over. It wasn't an ideal job, and there wasn't much room for romantic notions. In general, the whole dusky gray steel town didn't hold much mystique. My mother lived here because she was born here. Her family was here too, and they mostly held the idea that family was what you clung to so you didn't get lost in the great abyss. Sort of like people before they knew the world was round, who were afraid if you went too far you would fall off the edge.

I knew that men were good for the practical matters of money and house repairs, but not much else. At least none of the men here were good for much else. There were a few who held notions of something special—a high school teacher or a doctor who thought himself different and seemed to be looking for some unspecified uniqueness in others—but in general we tumbled forward without any illusions. Most girls lowered and lowered their standards until they accepted whatever grunting pass at love they got.

As a way for you to get closer, to get into my body, let me tell you that right now I am eating a lemon square, because the best snacks combine something tart and sweet. When I was eight I memorized the back of the box of Little Debbie Fudge Rounds. It was a beautiful family story about O. D. McKee, the founder of Little Debbie, and how he named the company after his four-year-old granddaughter. What I love most is that there is a story that goes along with your food.

If I could give you food to go along with this story I'm telling you, it would make me happy. A couple of suggestions in case you are hungry: raw brownie mix is a very nice treat; beets are surprisingly nice and underrated. I would make those for you, if given the chance.

Though I may seem different, fundamentally I am much like other women you may or may not have been with. I mean women you have seen naked, tasted, touched, been touched by, shared energy fields with, whispered deep things to, played sex games with, pretended you thought she was a dirty girl, held through the night, fucked. I have the same general parts as these women. I mean, I have a body and it functions. I guess you could say I AM a body, but then again I am not. At this moment, for example, my hand is making writing, but I am not sure where the thoughts I'm writing are coming from. My mother gave me the lemon square recipe.

## LEMON SQUARES

| | |
|---|---|
| 1 c. flour | 1/4 tsp. salt |
| 1/4 c. powdered sugar | 1/2 c. butter, softened |
| 2 eggs | 1 c. sugar |
| 2 tbsp. lemon juice | 1/2 tsp. baking powder |

Preheat oven to 350. Mix the flour, butter, and powdered sugar together. Press in ungreased square 8-inch baking dish. Press edges up on the sides 1/2 inch. Bake 20 minutes.

Mix regular sugar, eggs, lemon juice, baking powder, and salt together until light and fluffy. Pour this mixture over baked layer. Bake just until no indentation remains when touched in center, about 25 minutes. Let them sit awhile to cool before cutting them.

# THE LIBRARY

Even though it's a Saturday and I should be cleaning because my apartment is a pile of papers and clothes, I trek to the Riverton Public Library. I have a crush on an eighty-year-old man—a volunteer librarian named Hal Palm. The building is an old red brick firehouse converted in the '70s. The red bricks give me a feeling of comfort. Has there ever been an evil building built of red brick? Probably, yes—old factories with child workers chained to their machines—but here the brick feels like something solid and friendly.

I have been a regular library patron for about seventeen years. You had to be six to get your own card, and I got one as soon as I could. I have lost and misplaced many books over those years, but I still have the same card, with my name neatly typed on it and the edges soft and dirty.

Hal, my crush, is behind the desk checking out books, while behind him June Groff is looking over some papers with her reading glasses on. She still has the same mole on her chin that scared me as a child (and equated her, in my mind, with an evil witch), but she has developed a few more chins.

Hal smiles when he sees me. He is a good-looking man for his age, with his neatly trimmed beard and small wire eyeglasses and a still vigorous, if not hot, body. He is wearing a gray pinstriped suit and a bow tie. Of course, he is the most well-dressed man at the library. He told me he wears the suits because it's easier. He has so many left over from his years as a lawyer that it's a waste to just let them hang in his closet. After his wife died two years ago, he started volunteering at the library, and we became friends.

I feel an irritation on the back of my neck and reach inside the back of my shirt. It still has a tag in it, which I grab and, in one swift motion, rip out. I can't stand the feeling of tags on my skin.

Hal's eyebrows lift. They still have more pepper in them than salt and set off his amazing blue eyes. Maybe it's his eyes that make me have a crush on him. I feel like he is really looking at me, deep inside, and trying to figure out my motivations. Or maybe it's his intelligence—sharp and clear, even at his age, but never arrogant. A person smarter than you is always the sexiest thing.

Hal is studying a newspaper, *The New York Times*, I think. He points to an article. "I saved this for you," he says. "Did you hear about the mushroom poisonings?"

Poisoning? Did I eat something poisonous this morning? Have I eaten any poisons in the last few days? No. In the past year? No. I should be okay. "Where were they?"

"It's in California. Laotian immigrants. They confused *Amanita phalloides* with a kind of edible mushroom they eat in Laos."

Hal seems excited by the news. He's the kind of person who can take an intellectual interest in something like poisoning without feeling too much for the victims.

"I read about some cases like that last year." I lean over the newspaper and read more. "Yeah, *Amanita*. They don't have the death cap in Asia and they confuse them with an edible *Amanita* there. It's a common mistake. They aren't used to having to determine if the mushrooms are poisonous. It's a cruel trick of nature and geography. Did they die?"

June Groff looks at us like we're aliens and walks away. I feel like she still retains a disgust for me left over from my childhood, when I was a bad patron and never returned my books or returned them with water damage from the bathtub. She used to give me mini-lectures on book stewardship.

Hal doesn't seem to notice her leaving. He has a gift for ignoring social signs he doesn't want to pick up on. That's a good gift. I wish I had it.

"They'll probably make it," he says. "It looks like they'll need kidney transplants, though. Two kids and a mother."

Nobody besides June is paying our conversation any mind. There are a few people at the reading tables and a pregnant woman browsing in the expectant parents section. The library is functioning the way it should: information is being shared, and nobody cares who is looking at what. Except nosy June. To hell with her. She has moved across the room, but her body has the caught-in-the-headlights stillness of someone who is not budging an inch because it might interfere with their eavesdropping. No, we are not flirting, June. Are we?

"Who picked the mushroom? Who was the poisoner?"

"The uncle, but he was at work when they ate them. She made noodles with mushrooms. I'll photocopy the article for you."

"Wait, the guy who picked them didn't eat them? That's suspicious!"

I never eat mushrooms just in case a poison one accidentally gets in with a nonpoisonous one. I know this is unlikely, but not totally impossible, it would seem. The fact that mushrooms share this dual category of food and poison makes them especially frightening. They're something you can innocently eat, and then they'll turn on you and kill you—but then anything might turn on you and kill you. There is poison in eggs and chicken and beef and fast food.

"Do you know how much food poisoning there is?" I say. "Four million people get salmonella a year. We don't know how many cases of mad cow there are in Britain, and children are dying from eating Jack in the Box."

"Are you okay?" Hal asks. "Maybe I shouldn't have shown you this. I don't want you to get upset thinking about it."

I've admitted to Hal that sometimes I lie in bed and think about these things for hours. Sometimes I can't eat because I'm afraid everything is poisoned. Last night I made myself vomit because the clam linguine I had for dinner felt toxic. I don't know why I would eat clams anyway. It was all my fault for messing up and eating clams. They are bottom feeders, sucking up all the toxins in the poison river or ocean. Dioxins, mercury? Where did the clams even come from? It took just a few minutes to get them out of my system, and then I wasn't up all night feeling like I was going to die.

"I'm okay," I say.

"How's your job?" Hal asks, looking at me with concern.

"Same. Boring." What's there to really say about a job at the state inputing numbers for student loans into a database. I shouldn't be there. They all hate me and think I'm weird. Nobody wants to read a book or think or even open the newspaper. They only care about their grandkids and what's for dinner and the NBA. If I say any of these things then I'm just as boring as they are. Complaining is boring as hell.

"You're too smart for that job," Hal says, "but you'll find something else wonderful someday."

Am I too smart for that job? It's a kind of false logic, because if A was really too smart for job A, then A would not be at the job because their smartness would have moved them to job B or C or W. But A is at job A, and so they are not too smart for job A.

"I hope," I say quietly. What I don't say is I just want to survive without being poisoned so I can read and write my games and find love. If I could find my perfect lover, everything would be okay. And maybe Hal is the one. I am flirting with him. This is our way of flirting. Ah, I've got it now.

"Do you have any good books for me today?" I say, obviously the most flirtatious question ever. Hal will often set aside books for me behind the desk, new books or books he comes across that he knows I'll like.

"Nothing in particular," Hal says, "but what are you looking for?"

"I don't know. I'm in the kind of mood where nothing interests me," I say. With winter approaching and no love, my mood has been one where I struggle to poke my head out of my covers in the morning.

"I'm sure something will jump off the shelves if you look around," he says.

"Really? I doubt it." What's with Hal's cheerful mood today, I wonder. He's eighty and a widower. How the hell does he stay so peppy? But I want to feel cheerful. I want that feeling of hope.

"Just try to feel the books without looking," Hal says.

There is a disconnect between the way he looks, like a nice conservative gentleman, and what he is saying, which sounds like something you'd hear from a hippie.

"Feel the books without looking." I laugh. "How were you ever a lawyer when you talk like that?"

"I suppressed it. I was ultra-rational then, and now it's all coming back to haunt me. Every rationalist has an irrational side that turns around to bite them. Jung talks about that. He says rationalists are prone to some of the deepest irrationality because they distance themselves from it. He also says that after fifty, our repressed side comes forward; the feminine comes forward in the male."

I like Hal's ideas. I've tried to be attracted to dumb people just for their sweet good looks and soft skin, but it never works.

Hal runs his hands over the tops of some of the books on the counter, as if he were a blind man. "I remember someone from the country teaching me how to find four-leaf clovers," he says. "He was an expert at finding them, could find one in ten or fifteen minutes, and I couldn't find one in a whole afternoon. He told me you have to look without looking. I don't think he'd ever heard of zen, but it was a very zen approach. If you start counting the leaves, he told me, then you're in trouble. It's the same way with books. If you start reading the titles, it's too late. Just move around the books until one calls out to you. I've been doing it for forty years, and it works."

"Okay, I'm going to not look around."

"Give it a shot," Hal says. He looks so boyish sometimes with his shining eyes and quick smile.

I wander past the pregnant woman holding *What to Expect When You're Expecting* and the kids searching encyclopedias for information on dolphins and masturbation.

Last Saturday I went over to Hal's for tea. It was the first time we met outside the library. When I got to his house, he showed me his dead wife's garden and pointed to the snapdragons and the calendula and said that even when he did next to nothing to maintain them, the flowers his wife planted reseeded themselves and kept growing, though there were fewer each year. He said he isn't much of a gardener, but he plants violets each year because those were her favorites.

It was a beautiful late-summer day, and I sat in a wicker rocking chair, feeling like I could stay in the garden forever. While I relaxed, he went inside and brought out a silver tray with tea and ginger cookies. He told me how his wife was British, and he brought her to Riverton when they married because his family was here, and she never forgave him. I hope he was teasing. Maybe he wasn't.

He poured the tea slowly, adding tons of milk. I bit into a cookie.

"This ginger cookie really tastes like ginger," I said. "It tickles my nose."

"It should," he said. "I put four tablespoons of ginger in the dough."

"Impressive. You made them yourself."

Nothing frightens me about ginger. It's very safe. I felt like I was really relaxing for the first time in a long time, like I was being taken care of.

"You can't buy real ginger cookies in Riverton. I miss teatime. I came home every day to teatime for fifty years."

The roses were blooming like wild pink pompoms, and I noticed some ants crawling on them. Why did roses always have ants, especially on the unopened buds? Did ants help open them up? Hal picked a pink snapdragon and pushed the mouth of it open, the way my aunt would always do. I picked a yellow one and started pushing the mouth open, and it felt kind of sexy. It looked like the lips of a pussy. Holding the snapdragon and looking at Hal's earlobes, which have become elongated and lumpy, the way old people's do, I became a little aroused. I thought about asking if I could touch his earlobes, but it didn't seem right.

"Can I tell you about a dream?" I asked.

"I love hearing about dreams," he said. I know he does, and I have started trying to remember mine for him.

"I had a weird dream that kind of scared me. There was a family of spiders that moved into my house, and when I tried to get them out, they kept multiplying. They were in the closet and under the carpets."

"That's interesting," he said. "Jung said everyone in the dream is you."

"So you're saying that I'm a whole family of spiders? That's a bit disgusting. Would I bite people?"

"Maybe, or weave webs. Actually the spider is a very powerful symbol and not all bad. Jung thought the spider represented connection and creativity. It's a good sign."

"Sure," I said. "That's why people hate them so much and children run away—because they are a symbol of creativity."

"Could be," Hal said and grinned. "And power. Nobody likes power very much."

I put my head back in the chair, considering the possibility that I was a whole family of spiders and that it was a good thing to be.

When I got up to leave, Hal took my hand to help me out of the rocker, and I thought maybe he would keep hold of my hand and lead me to the bedroom. He would say, "I haven't been with a woman in a long time," and then he would gently undress me and tell me how smart and beautiful I am. I know this would be disgusting for most people because of his age, but I like the way he looks. I like his gray hair, and the way that I can see the veins through his hands (like the insides of his body are thinking of coming out), and his bright blue eyes, the kind that have just gotten brighter with age. I think about him touching me. I imagine his penis as saggy and soft and how I would just sit on top of it and rock back and forth and it wouldn't matter if it got hard or not. No thrusting, just rubbing. He would touch me like he could really feel my skin, like my skin was an important ingredient to him. He probably hasn't had sex with anyone since his wife died, and maybe long before, since she was sick and he was taking care of her. To me sex isn't about being attractive in a glamorous way, it's about making some kind of connection, and if I could connect with Hal, I could connect with a different way of looking at the world. If I had sex with him, I would be having sex with all of his years of experience and the knowledge he has of death, the knowledge that life isn't going to last forever. Most young people know nothing about death.

Whenever I really like someone, I imagine them dying. For each person the death is something different. Hal I imagine having a heart attack when I'm in bed with him, or maybe he starts coughing up blood. Coughing up blood I could deal with; I like body fluids. I think that you don't really love someone unless you want their fluids dripped all over you. I like to think of myself as the kind of lover who could deal with all body fluids, but really I haven't had that much experience with anything but a few handfuls of semen.

I remember one summer there was a special ed girl who came to camp with a bunch of us from town, and at the end of camp the counselor realized that she had been saving all of her dirty menstrual pads in a suitcase, and she was going to take them home with her. On the one hand it seemed totally bizarre, but it also made a weird kind of sense to me—the attachment she had to her body and what came out of it. I think lovers should have the same kind of attachment to each other's bodies. I wouldn't like someone who thought my bleeding was messy or horrible; I could accept emptying Hal's bedpan if I were in love.

I wander around the library, not looking. Like with most public libraries, the shelves are mostly filled with practical books—books on how to get a divorce, file for bankruptcy, invest in the stock market, make a stone wall, cook a Thai dinner, get along with your sister (mother, brother, father, husband, and kids). It's exhausting. But mixed in with the practical books are a few dreamier, philosophical ones. After his wife died, Hal donated most of his books to the library and cataloged them himself. He added his books on mythology, anthropology, psychology, alchemy, and the occult.

As I cruise the shelves, I try to put myself in the zenlike state he described. I pass books on philosophy, psychology, something about alcoholics, mandalas, being your own therapist, plant identification, bird sightseeing trips in Costa Rica (my mind goes there a second, but then pulls back)—I try to just feel the book without looking too much, like the four-leaf clover. I move through the books like I would a forest, noticing but not hunkering down, taking it all in with my senses. The bright blue words on the spine of a white book pop out at me. It's more the shape of the words than the words themselves that lure me in: *The Poetics of Space.* I open the cover of the book. There is a white bookplate with gold letters: *Donated to the Riverton Public Library in memory of Lydia Palm.* That was Hal's wife. The book feels wonderful in my hand, and my boredom is replaced by a slight inquisitiveness. How can there be a poetics of space? What does it mean? I open to a random page: "Wardrobes with their shelves, desks with their drawers, and chests with their false bottoms are veritable organs of the secret psychological life."

*Veritable organs.* This is my book. Organs of the secret psychological life.

*game three*

# EARLOBES

I have long felt that earlobes are too sensual to be seen by everyone. They scream sex with their rounded knobs of pleasure. How can people just go out in public with that part of their body exposed—so soft, so ripe, so sensitive? Maybe that's one of the reasons I am attracted to Hal. I love old people's earlobes. They start to get saggy and lose some of their elasticity, but they become more tender, and soft like bread dough.

Come closer. Touch my belly. Feel my fat under your fingertips and inhale the strange smell of my breath and between my legs and under my arms. Let me sniff you and figure you out. Let me remember your smell for days and then forget it because smell can't really be remembered, only experienced. I am falling into your scent, the way we move toward each other, me telling my story. I show you the scar on my ankle from when I tried to chop wood at seven—every body part with a history. Maybe it's selfish and maybe it's wrong and maybe it's magical, this giving of myself to you. I don't know. I don't know. Come closer.

My fear of poisoning started in childhood. I'm not sure why, but I remember first being afraid of vitamins. I thought there was something not right about those colorful tablets with their chalky texture, even if they looked like the Flintstones. They contained iron and everything else mixed together, and I had a sense that they were small doses of death. I remember my mother giving me the vitamin, and the feeling of dread inside of me. I waited a few hours to die and eventually forgot about dying after I didn't. Since then, I often wait to die.

After vitamins, my fear moved to a sense that something was in my throat. I had the feeling that phlegm was building up there, deep down, and I coughed a lot. It wasn't something I could control. I started to worry about the germs in tissues and on pieces of paper and in the streets, and there were diseases and poisons in the news all the time. This was after the Tylenol scare, when everyone was thinking about tampering, how someone could just slip poison into our food or drugs and we wouldn't know. How dangerous it seemed to put all of these substances in our open mouths.

I also became afraid of cans whose contents might be spoiled, of botulism, and contamination by blood. If my mother was cleaning the sink and got some Comet on the counter, I thought the Comet would get into my food and I would swallow it and it would kill me. I spent many nights thinking about what I had eaten that day. I would spill something and clean it up, and then I would fear that I got the cleaning fluid on me, or I would be walking and pick up something I found on the street—maybe a vase or a pair of shoes—but then think that maybe there was a deadly chemical on that vase. Maybe someone was making deadly chemicals in their garage, like mercury, and it was on the vase I picked up and could kill me just by my touching it. Maybe it would kill me right away, or maybe it would take a long time. It might give me cancer or some other disease, and I would never know the source. I am also always aware of toxins in the environment. I know that we are all polluting and killing ourselves a little more every day, so perhaps my anxiety is a logical and right way to feel.

These fears, believe it or not, are part of my body, so if you are bored with them then forget about becoming my lover.

# THE SUPERMARKET

It's Sunday, and I'm headed out to the supermarket, and Blackie 2 keeps trying to get into my apartment. This happens every time I open my door. My landlady, who is also my neighbor, has more cats than anyone I know—so many that I have generic names for them like Blackie 1 and 2, Scrubs, Whitie, Cally, Spots, Darkest One, Cutest One (which changes sometimes), and there are always others I don't recognize showing up. I think Fran, my landlady, is a cat hoarder. I read about the condition, which is a form of obsessive compulsiveness that strikes primarily older, single women, resulting in their keeping an excessive number of cats, often more than they can possibly take care of.

With Fran I don't think it's a problem. Not like a woman in Indiana I read about who had hundreds of cats that filled her house and some would die and there were corpses of cats lying around and cats eating each other in a terrible cannibalism. No, Fran has a mild case.

Fran lives in the house in front of my place, or to look at it like most people would, I live in the tiny in-law apartment behind her home. Before I moved in, my apartment was also filled with cats. I know because it still smells like cat pee and all the wooden baseboards are scratched up and I find cat-food tins when I dig in the backyard—Fancy Feast or Cat Chow, the sweet faces of the felines ripped off and muddied. Now Fran has about twelve cats. She feeds them in a big cat trough, and whenever I go in her house, there are always one or two sitting on the chair, the floor, the couch, or the counter. I think if she had her way, she would have kept the whole studio apartment just for the cats, but she needed the money.

She told me once that if she had enough money she would buy an island for abandoned cats. I'm not sure how that would work. I guess she would feed them, or maybe she would pick an island with mouse abundance. She described a dream she'd had in which she needed to save cats all over the world, and all of the hungry and injured cats—cats in Asia and in Mexico and in places where cats were ragged and abused—were all following her, and she was taking them to a place that was clean and pure and safe. Kind of like the pied piper.

I wanted to say, "So you were like the messiah of the cats?" but I didn't. That would have been mean, and I like her. Fran is in her early sixties, works at the pharmacy in town, and doesn't have any children. Sometimes I find her sad, and at other times I find her and her cats to be living in a beautiful parallel universe. She mothers me a little, but in a distant way, like a liberated mother who would encourage you to go backpacking in India. Fran was an adventurer herself once, and lived in Brazil for three years before she got married and divorced and started caring for her mother with Alzheimer's. She cared for her mother for nine years.

Her mother passed on, but Fran never resumed any of her own adventures, and now she has her cats. I hear her talking to them sometimes when I pass the apartment. "Lovely," she says, "be a kind girl and scratch your post and not my legs," or "Sam, I like to take five sugars in my tea, and I don't care what the doctor says." In Egypt, she told me, cats were worshipped, and if you killed a cat you were condemned to death. She said she thought we should still have a law like that, which made me wonder a little about her mental health, but I don't think she would really enforce that law, and she's always nice to me. She has a nickname for me, *the wandering child*, even though I never go anywhere but into the city for work. I wander around town a bit, I guess.

There is a game I call *find something of interest in even the most boring place*. Sometimes I play it by walking and looking for things on the street, and sometimes I go to the store. It's impossible to imagine what I could possibly find interesting at the supermarket today, but that makes the game challenging.

Often I feel like this town is in me in some strange way, that I could open a part of my brain and roll out a map. Riverton consists of: one grocery store that is known for its deli (where you can buy chicken pot pie, red beet eggs, and eight kinds of potato salad); a flower shop; a thrift store with blouses for two dollars; one nice restaurant in an old Victorian house; five dingy bars; one strip place called the Pink Pussycat; two Dollar Generals; some barber shops; a place for old folks to go for day care when they get senile; a few pizza places; four elementary schools and one high school; one doll hospital (where a ninety-year-old woman will sew the eyes and arms back on your doll); eight churches, each of which is only a shade or two of different from the others; one synagogue; and the old theater that has been around forever and somehow hasn't been turned into a church or a lodge like the old theaters in nearby small towns. There is a project down by the river where poor people live, and one rundown shack where a whole family lives, and then the downtown, and then the rows and rows of small houses with aluminum siding and small yards where people raise families. That's where I was raised. My apartment now is in the older section, near the cemetery where the founder of Riverton is buried, his grave facing a different direction than all of the others.

That's the town without emotional resonance, stripped to its bare markers, as an outsider who wanders in would see it. But underneath that map is the map of my memories of Riverton.

Concerning the churches, there is one scandal involving a choir director and minister, and another involving a youth director and a married man in the congregation. They both involve sex, and you could probably imagine them for yourself. At age five, I almost lost my life in front of a church. One hot summer day when I tried to roll down the window I pulled the door open instead, and my mother, from the driver's seat, reached over—one hand on the wheel and the other catching me by the heel—and pulled me back in before I hit pavement.

There is the abandoned land where the old coal plant used to be before they built the nuclear plant alongside the slow brown river, land strangled by cattails, bursting with squirrels and groundhogs. There is the bungalow where my grandparents lived before they died, and another house on the bad side of the tracks where my other grandmother lived. There is the place where my father told me he shot a cat in a tree, and the place I went after my father left—a forsythia bush down by the river. I hid for one whole afternoon, lying on an army blanket, hoping someone would find me. Sometimes all the history feels like a dull weight. The ghosts of my grandparents are probably watching me reproachfully from somewhere in town right now.

In the winter everything is gray, and in the summer it is green, a green so bright it feels like it's nibbling your toes and multiplying fast, so fast, only to be wiped out by frost. This cycle is sad and obliterates my hopes of doing something that may last. Despite this sense of despair, or maybe because of it, the town and I are connected. I could be blindfolded and dropped somewhere, and when I was taken out of the car I would know where I was, or if I could peek out of the corner of the blindfold and catch a glimpse of a house or a building or an empty lot with a rusting Pinto, I could piece the clues together and pinpoint my location. That's what it means to belong someplace, I guess, and it is a terrible and beautiful thing.

Here the Susquehanna River flows into the Swatara Creek. Some days I think the only good thing about the town is the river, and sometimes I don't even know if that's good. The town is divided into river people and non-river people. There are some who spend all the time they can from spring until fall in boats, fishing and swimming, or on islands where they have summer cabins, and others who never go near the water. The river was a mystery to me as a child because I never went out on it. We weren't river people. Who knows what kinds of chemicals are floating in there? Emptyings from the steel factories and the coalfields and everything else that was pumped or shipped out of this area only to leave us depressed and useless, industrial has-beens.

I walk to the BigTown food store. It was big excitement when Big-Town went 24-hour, and not just because of the deli. They have a campaign to bring exotic fruit to the people of Riverton. For example, on the produce case there is a short description of the star fruit—a cross

between a grape and an apple that can be used in desserts and salads—
and what it can bring into your life: variety, vitamin C, a pleasing bev-
erage garnish. I look at the produce display and think of bringing a new
fruit into my life and what it might mean. On the one hand, each fruit
has a history that I want to share in: geography, ways of being eaten,
customs, and possibly mythology. On the other hand, there are so many
unanswered questions. Who picks it, and what do they eat for breakfast?
What are they wearing on their feet? It comes to me through so many
hands that by the time it reaches me I can barely see its starting point in
the soil. And despite the little description, I don't really know what to do
with it. Most people here, I'm sure, do not buy the new fruit. I'm not sure
they even see it. They buy apples and bananas and oranges. Women have
set patterns of shopping: the ones with children in tow avoid known
temptations and eye diversions; the young ones throw in their cart whatever is fastest, easiest, microwavable, prepackaged, and allows them
to feel like they are eating something nutritious; the older ones have
routines so regular that when the clerks rearrange the aisles they become
so flummoxed it becomes a topic of conversation at card club.

When I go to BigTown, I'm looking for something interesting. I've
always had this fantasy that I would find something unique at the grocery store, something magical. The hard part is recognizing it. How do
you know if something is special? I trudge through the aisles like an ele-
phant, dawdling, marking slight differences in brands and any attempts
at originality. Today there is a change in the ethnic foods section, with
the addition of guava paste and molé and tortillas in more varieties:
corn, wheat, spinach, small, large, grande. Although star fruit might be
too much, I think I should start adding molé to my diet. It's like eating
chocolate on chicken, right?

I go to the small book section and page through the paperbacks. I
have a fantasy that someday I'll find an arcane and elusive book, a rare
book with mysterious information about how to live my life or how to
discover magic or about a secret cult in the next town over. But all of
the books are romances, best sellers, mysteries, and diet programs. I
leaf through a book about a doctor solving a murder, a book about three

sisters from the South who are all having trouble with men, and a book about a woman who sleeps with a lot of men and then finds Mr. Right. None of them excite me. Unfortunately BigTown is the only place in Riverton that even sells books, except for the library at their annual sale. Out of desperation, I've bought some BigTown books about angels or crystals, looking for a hidden message in them, but I never found one.

The potato chip aisle is my favorite place. Even though chips are evil, I love the variety of brands. Pennsylvania has a unique relationship with potato chips. While in other states Frito-Lay has the absolute monopoly, in Pennsylvania potato chips are still made by local companies (in a manner most tasty) like Utz, Moyer's, and Bickel's. My personal favorite is Utz, which makes a chip that's utterly light yet not dry, with an addictive, slightly oily taste. Bickel's are heavy-duty kettle-fried chips that my mother likes. When I was growing up, we always had potato chips on Sundays at my grandmother's house, and my one aunt's sole job, as I saw it, was to make sure that the chip basket—a wicker basket with a thin layer of napkins lining the bottom—stayed full. My aunt acquired that job because her place at the table was next to the closet where the potato chips were kept. It is odd how we acquire work based on where we are, physically, in a given moment.

Since I am walking and didn't find anything magical, I leave BigTown with only four items: potato chips, star fruit, beets, and tampons.

On my way out of the store, I catch sight of a man—balding, graying, in a black coat—at the edge of the parking lot, walking away at a fast pace. A cold feeling moves up my body. I walk quickly toward him. As he turns, I only catch the side of his face and the back of his head, but there is a familiarity there, the line of his nose, something in his mouth—older, but him. It's my father. I think it's my father. Am I insane? My father has been missing for eleven years, and what would he be doing at the BigTown on a Saturday afternoon, and if he were in Riverton, why wouldn't he be at home?

I continue following the man, who is walking rapidly toward the park. He is getting out something from his pocket, a pack of cigarettes, and lighting one. The last time I saw my father, he smoked Camels and chewed tobacco—twice the cancer risk, twice the fun. My mother complained about it every day, and I became a young crusader too. I even wore a sign around my neck at home for a week that read, *You are reducing my life expectancy*. I am about fifty feet behind him. I cannot see him clearly, only the back of his head. His walk is heavy but fast, as if he is pulling a great weight but in a hurry to get it somewhere. As if when he gets to that place, wherever that might be, he can drop the weight. I could call his name and see if he answers. I could say *Dad*, but that would feel rusty in my mouth, like a penny that I've sucked on, and besides, he might turn because he's someone else's dad.

I follow him a few blocks, past some residential streets. A small boy in the driveway of a house is dribbling a ball, then shoots and misses the basket. I pass the soft-serve ice cream place, Scoops, where nobody goes in the winter, but today there are two families sitting on the swings eating soft cones with jimmies on top. I follow him into the town park, which was built next to the creek, where young couples go to make out and families go to picnic. I'm crazy. I should go home, but what if it's him and I miss this chance? I know in my mind it can't be him, but I follow anyway. What if it is my father and he turns to me and says, "Well, you finally found me, kid."

He stops at a bench facing the river. I am so close behind him now that when he stops, he notices and swivels around. I see his full face now, older than my father's would be, with a sharper nose and bushier eyebrows and slightly frightening eyes—the face of a stranger. He looks at me for a second and then turns away, gets out the bag that he bought at BigTown, a sack of bird seed, and starts feeding the birds, who quickly gather. Those weren't my father's eyes. Those eyes were dark, empty sockets. Even though my father could be mean and make you feel stupid, he had the quick, playful eyes of a child.

I sit down at a bench nearby. The river is the color of muddy thoughts and despair. Where do you go when you disappear? There have been other times I've thought I've seen my father like this, and I promised myself not to believe it anymore. Even if it was my father, what would I do? I would want to ask him where he's been all of these years and why he disappeared. I would want to hit him over and over, and if I were in the park and there was an empty Rolling Rock bottle on the ground, like there is here, I might pick up the bottle and smash it over his head, and then he might die, and what would be the difference anyway between wondering if he is dead and then finding out he is not dead but killing him? What is the difference between all of the nights I wanted to see his face again and the other nights when I have hated him so much for leaving us, I wished him dead? If he is alive, I want to kill him.

I remember the part in Hansel and Gretel when the father takes the children into the woods to lose them. I always thought that was the greatest betrayal, but what is worse—to lose your children or disappear from them? At least, if you lose them, they can hold onto the idea that it was a mistake.

I head home, past the old steel plant that's been shut down for eight years, where my father used to work. Gray husks of buildings stretch away from the town like large ships, the canals they used to move the steel now shining with peacock-colored oils, abandoned machinery resting here and there, and then a surprise: a bright sky-blue chimney that offsets the drab color of the buildings. There is a cat walking on the railroad ties, and I think he must be happy to have the whole place to himself. Progress.

*game four*

# HANSEL AND ME

This is one of my fantasies. I don't know why they don't make sense except in a way that pleases my throat, behind my eyelids, the inside of my mouth.

This morning our father, the logger, sent us deep into the woods to find mushrooms. He told us that we were looking for morels, but he didn't tell us what they looked like. He just said to bring them home. We didn't ask any questions. He has a temper. So we walk farther and farther but we don't find them and we know what is going on. We are not fools. Our parents have been itching to get rid of us ever since they met at the country line dance. Your mother is what my mother, who is now dead, would call a floozy or a slut. My father is crazy about fucking her. They send us outside to play and don't call us until after dark, and if we come home before then, the door is locked.

I am afraid they have sent us into the woods to be eaten by the witch. I have heard stories in town that there's a woman in the forest who was previously called a witch. My English teacher says we are not supposed to use the term witch anymore because it's derogatory. Your mother just calls her an old whore. I've heard she looks like a vulture and she eats children and she dances naked at night and she has sex with men who go there and if she likes them she lets them live and if she doesn't she kills them. I have to admit I am very impressed by the witch. She does whatever she wants. I like the fact that she dances naked. I like her killing the lovers. I wouldn't even mind if she killed some children, but not us. Maybe our father went there and had sex with her. Maybe she didn't like him, but instead of killing him, she made him promise to send her his children.

This is the way I think. This is my dark mind. You, Hansel, have more level thoughts. You have logical thoughts. But we share a certain hunger. We share a certain intimacy based on hunger. I know that you are alive, and you know that I am alive. We know that being alive is not such a certain thing and that we would do anything to stay that way. That is our pact.

We walk all day, deeper and deeper into the forest, and instead of talking about the fact that we are in danger, we talk about food. We have been hungry for a long time, so this is our favorite game. We talk about mashed potatoes with deep pools of butter, foie gras, caviar, and filet mignon. We talk about the kind of pastries called petit fours that we read about in a book. I'm not sure what those pastries are, but in the book they provided such pleasure for the girl and boy who were eating them, the sort of pleasure few other things can provide. Sometimes we describe food to each other for hours. In our house, we eat only turnips, Wonder bread, Cheez Whiz, and ring bologna. Our diet is limited, and therefore our imagination is unlimited.

You are an attractive boy. I saw that when you first moved in. Me, I'm not much of a looker, but you are sort of a boy-god—the kind of child that many men in the trailer park want to be a big brother to. Your hair is light and curly, and you have long eyelashes like a girl's. If you weren't my stepbrother, I would be in love with you. I am in love with you anyway, maybe.

"What should we have for lunch?" I ask. We are sitting under a tree and taking a break from our fruitless hunting.

"We'll have lamb with plum sauce, camembert cheese with blackberry pie, and red wine," you say.

I have never tasted any of these foods except blackberry pie, and that was at Denny's after Grandma's funeral, and I don't think it was the freshest.

"No," I say, "let's have lobster thermidor, sautéed escargot, cauliflower soup with white truffle oil, and warm chocolate pudding." I have been studying old cooking magazines to impress you.

All day we have been leaving a path of bread scraps, just in case. Held in my hands all day, the loaf becomes sticky and dirty. When my real mother was still alive and she drove me past the Stroehmann bakery, we always stopped and sniffed the air to catch the yeasty smell of the rows and rows of rolls and bread, which we sometimes caught a glimpse of through the factory window, lying next to each other on endless trays like small white bodies. Being with my mother at such a time was special. Eating bread in the presence of one's mother is a very important thing. Now that my mother is dead, I have no one to eat bread in front of who matters.

You are hungry, and I give you some of the bread that has been in my hand all day—Wonder bread pressed into the shape of my fingers. You eat it in little nibbles.

After lunch we look for the mushrooms again, but we don't find them. In my pocket, I keep a piece of my dead mother's nightgown. I take it out and smell it from time to time, but I have sniffed it so often that I can't tell if it still has her smell or I am imagining it. I remember how I sat on her lap, how she made me rice pudding from scratch and combed my hair, her fingers tickling my neck and making me feel like I was so light I might float away.

At dusk we try to kill a rabbit. You throw a rock at it, and it runs away. Instead we find a turtle. You brought some matches, and we build a fire. We cook the turtle on a stick over the fire. The turtle is still alive when we start to cook it. It withdraws into its shell at first, but then when it realizes the danger, it tries to escape. I can't stand to watch it struggle. I think how horrible it must be to be cooked alive in your own shell—to have your own body turned into the oven that is cooking you; there is no way out, and going deeper inside only makes it worse.

I only eat berries. You save some of the turtle for me in case I'm hungry later. You say maybe I'll want some in the morning. I don't know then that in the morning, starving, I will cram the cold turtle into my mouth and chew and chew on the rubbery flesh. It will taste wonderful.

As it gets dark, I become scared and see a woman with an axe in the shadows of the leaves.

"No," you say, "it's not real." You have a way of separating hallucination from reality—a way of separating the two like wheat from chaff. You are my winnower.

"Are you afraid?" you ask me, your voice comforting.

"Yes," I say, "but I'm always afraid. Why do you think they sent us here?" I ask. I always ask you things that I know.

"So they could be free." I like how you say it. When you phrase it that way, it doesn't sound so bad. Maybe my father does love me some, but just loves her more. Maybe he is setting me free too. Though really I think he is an asshole.

"But we're children," I say.

"Exactly," you say. "My mother never wanted to have children. I was an accident. She tells me that sometimes when I get on her nerves. She just wants to be alone with Phil."

Phil is my father. You have refused to call him *Father*, of course. I never thought of him as much of a looker, but she is all over him.

"Yes," I say, "they just want to have sex and listen to country music."

"And smoke joints."

"I should be sad, but I just feel scared," I say.

Now that it is dark, the game is over. Maybe a bear will come and maul us or a mad killer who waits for children, and there is still the witch to consider.

"I hate them both," you say.

"Me too," I say, but really I do not feel hate so much as a terrible, terrible sickness. Sometimes I wish I could be as angry as you. It seems to protect you, like a shield their shit just bounces off of. "What do you think will happen to us?" I ask.

"They think we'll die, but we won't," you say.

*Yes,* I think. *We won't.* Somehow the fact that we have said it makes me feel a sense of relief, as if, now, admitting what we are up against, we have a chance.

We do things in the dark. It isn't exactly sex, but you push your body against mine so there is no room between us, and you put your hands between my legs but don't move them. You just press against me, and it soothes me.

I whisper, "Will you always be here?"

"Yes," you say.

Even though we are miserable, I am less miserable with you.

I dream of the bread that I put on the path, and each scrap of dry bread is rising again like yeasty dough and baking itself into a full, warm loaf. We scoop them all up and put them in our baskets. We can't resist smelling each one, like the bellies of babies.

If you weren't my stepbrother, I would want to marry you.

In the morning, we anticipate seeing the witch, but instead we find a house that is empty. The house is made of candy, and we start eating it, our hands full of sticky chocolate siding with raspberries, marshmallow cobblestones, peanut butter steps, and peppermint windowpanes. Trying for a moment of forethought, I say, "Should we be eating someone else's house?"

"It's candy," you say—always the one with the right answer. "It's meant to be eaten." Candy does seem by definition intended to be eaten, but in this case it is also a building material. In any case, physical hunger and our childish natures win out.

Later the witch comes home and is angry with us. "This is a gross destruction of private property," she says. "You'll have to pay with your lives."

We identify her as a witch because she is old and ugly. Even so, she is not someone we will burn at the stake or torture to find out her pact with Satan. That has been done in the past. I know that from my English teacher, who seems to love talking about what she calls The Burning Times. She says the witch is a scapegoat for men's fear of women. But this is a real witch, and there is real reason for fear.

After the first night, I realize that the witch does not want to kill me. She only wants to kill you. She tells me that men are the real problem and that she will groom me to be a witch like her. I pretend that I have turned on you and am in love with the witch. Her name is Evelyn. I mend her nightgowns. I clean the house. I wash her underwear, which have the foul smell of old folks' urine. All the while I am plotting how to kill Evelyn. She puts you in a cage, where you are supposed to grow fat like a lamb. She has the key in a locket around her neck; she's so old-fashioned. I can't figure out how to get it. She fusses over me and tells me how pretty I am. She combs my hair, and I feel her old, scaly fingers running over my scalp and touching the skin on my neck and shoulders. It makes me shudder. I don't know if she wants to eat me or make love with me. It all feels the same.

I cook meals and feed them to you, but when she leaves, you make yourself throw up into a yellow Tupperware container, and I take it outside. I dig holes in the yard and bury your vomit. I uncover many bones. Some of them look human.

One day when Evelyn returns from one of her trips, she decides it's time to eat you. She asks me to heat the oven, and I realize I need to act now. I need to be brave, because what will I do if she kills you? I tell her that the flue in the oven is stuck and that I can't get the heat that I need to bake you. She puts her head into the oven to see, and I push her from behind. She struggles, but I am stronger. She turns toward me and looks more vulnerable than expected. More like an old woman than a witch, with her body bent over and her hair turned gray and a beet stain on the front of her dress. I push nonetheless. I push and think of you. She fights back, but she is old and I am young. Of course, the smell of human flesh burning is horrible. I do what I have to do, though she might have been misunderstood. Perhaps I should have tried harder to love her so she would change inside.

But you are saved, and we push our children's bodies together. We gorge on the house, and I run my hands through your sticky, lollipop hair. You put your candied lips against mine. You put your gummy-worm tongue in my mouth. Our parents have ditched us, the witch is dead: what's there to lose? Your hands run up my dress. I touch you and lick your eyelids. We have sex like we think men and women do.

After that day we see we can't go back home and we can't be together. It would be too complicated, and we just want to forget everything that happened. I'm taken away by child protective services and adopted by a gay couple. We have a "don't ask, don't tell" policy. They don't ask me about my childhood, and I don't ask them if they're really sure they'll stay together forever and ever. We never eat Wonder bread, and I finally get to taste truffle oil. And you? I don't know where you go. We learned from our childhood that there is no looking back; the trail is already gone. One day I hear that you lied about your age and got a job at the bread factory. After that, when I am eating a piece of bread, I imagine you were the one who baked it, sealed it, or at the very least loaded the pallet onto the truck.

# COMPROMISE

I pass the copy machine at my terrible job without anyone noticing me. Nobody is copying anything yet. I pass Betty Merringer's desk and the row of cubicles where all of the secretaries sit. It's still early, and most people are filling up on caffeine in the break room, but I'm already full. I'm smooth and rolling and this is generally the only part of the day when I feel good, because I've reached my caffeine high.

Though I say I hate my job, part of me loves it because nobody bothers me and I just do the things they tell me and don't have to think. They don't talk to me. I go to a desk and get my work for the day, and then I sit in my cubicle putting the numbers in the computer. I compare lists of numbers for loans and input data. Then, at the end of the day, I give my work over to Betty Merringer, and she checks it off.

I have been obsessed with Betty, in an anthropological sense, since I started working here. Betty has short, utilitarian hair. She is overweight (in the hips and butt mostly) and does her work without complaining. Betty is in her early fifties and has a son and daughter, both of whom also have children. She is your classic proud grandmother and brings photos to the office of the kids eating, singing, standing, playing in sand, playing in grass, and kissing her. Betty's life strikes me as boring. But she doesn't seem bored with it. And that is where the mystery lies—where I try and see what within her life makes it seem satisfactory. When I think of her life and swimming around in it, I feel a sense of drowning. I guess it's all about my dread that I might be still working here when I'm her age, having done nothing exciting with my life. Betty is what I fear becoming, and that's why she makes me feel so awful. But maybe her life isn't so bad. Maybe if I let myself drown, I'd see what is there.

Betty seems to enjoy her job, even though she has cancer, and in my petty mind I wonder if the job gave it to her, maybe something in the vent system—asbestos? Her cancer is in remission, though, and we all celebrated at the office with pink cupcakes.

Lots of young people come and go from this office, but I stay. I stay because the work doesn't eat the free space in my brain—which pleases me—leaving it open, like the white filling inside a Hostess cupcake. Inside the dark cake, like this dark office, is a place of white and lightness, where anything is possible. So though I am a prisoner here and on many days feel like I am serving time and my life is meaningless, on other days I feel like I am the white fluffy icing, hiding out inside.

Betty is the opposite of everything I hope to be. She loves her job, she loves her grandkids, she loves doing crafty things. Her kitchen, where she hosts a boring annual Christmas party, is decorated in the traditional country style, which means lots of baskets, flowers, roosters, and potholders that have things on them like a country boy giving a country girl a peck on the cheek. There is no end to the abundance of country clutter in her house. I don't mean old stuff; it's all new stuff that has been made to look old or made with this idea of creating a perfect cozy country home. Betty, of course, is nice, and I chafe against her niceness like the rope that it is, the rope of safety and being a good woman. I know everyone is different, but it's still a conundrum to me that people can live lives that seem so dull and still be happy.

At my desk stands Mr. Rollins, my superior, whom I refer to in my mind as Beaker because he reminds me of that Muppets character who was very tall and pink. He is a flushed man with a moustache, in his sixties, thin and observant. He seems very slick and almost car-salesman sticky with his way of making you feel like you do everything wrong and he does everything right, but in a nice way. He smiles at me. His foot is tapping on the floor, and it has an almost musical quality to it, as if he might become Fred Astaire and swoop me over to the copier, but his foot does not match his forehead, which, for all of his painted-on smile, is tense and lined and has the look of someone who is trying too hard.

"Claudia," he says. "Great to see you."

I don't know how long he has been hovering, waiting for me, but I am not bothered in the way I might be at other jobs. I never get in trouble for not working hard enough, only for not doing things right. We are a pure bureaucracy here and don't have much reason to hurry, but the perfectionistic tedium shows its hydra heads at even my level. Right papers on the right desks, right boxes filled in.

"Good morning, Mr. Rollins. How are you?"

Mr. Rollins smiles with his mouth very stiff, like he has had plastic surgery, but I don't think he has. His face has been shaped into this form by his actions.

"Great, thanks. Claudia, I wanted to talk to you about something."

When he says my name, I feel an urge to make him stop—it feels like an invasion—but you can't stop people from saying your name.

"You've been doing a great job, really excellent, but I'm afraid that you might be confused about some of the protocol concerning the state forms for student loan deferral and who the correct person to give the forms to is, in the event of deferral for medical emergency."

He loves to catch me on some small technical glitch. He loves to catch everyone and then lecture them on procedure. I think his brain must look like a form by now, and I feel sorry for him about that. Beaker is single and pours all of this life energy into this job. He cares about it way deeper than this job has any right to be cared about.

My mind starts to wander as he tells me information. I imagine that he and Sandy Geary in customer service are having an affair and that they slip into the broom closet to have sex. This kind of fantasy is disturbing and satisfying. I picture him having sex—that fake, waxy smile never leaving his face—and then at the end he says, "Great job." I imagine that she gets pregnant, and then, when her husband finds out, he is angry because the doctor told him that he was infertile, so he knows it is a bastard child. But she is secretly happy because she's going to have a baby. These thoughts all slip through my head in a few seconds. I am good at this game. I am infinitely good at imagining I am anywhere but where I am. Luckily, at this job, even if I don't pay attention, I can never get behind because it is all about repetition. Of course, I know everything Beaker is lecturing me on, but I nod anyway.

Then, as if by a miracle, a young guy I have never seen before, who has light and dark hair, walks up to Mr. Rollins and says, "Hi, my name's Luke. I'm from Excel Services."

Great, a temp. Beaker is called away to the higher duty of finding work for him. I love temps because now Beaker will channel all his energy for telling people precisely how to do things into the temp, who will have to listen and take notes and do things exactly, or they will not be back tomorrow. Nothing ever changes here. (There is a note thumbtacked up in the break room with a name on it of someone who hasn't worked here for five years, and nobody removes it.) Temps are fresh blood. I am attracted to them for that reason, and also because I realize they will leave, so I can tell them things I don't want other people to know. Sometimes I have three- or five-week friendships with them. Most people at work look down on temps because they don't have full-time jobs with benefits. Benefits, my coworkers think, are the pinnacle of existence. But I envy the temps because they get to leave.

I've been at this job for three years, ever since I graduated from community college with a two-year degree. I never thought I would be here longer than a few months. After community college, I was going to go on for my BA, but I couldn't make up my mind where to go, and my mom knew someone who worked at the state and got me this job, a kind of mixed blessing, I guess. In my more depressed moments, I think of it like offering someone who is thirsty a cup of hemlock.

# HAROLD AND MAUDE

I called Hal up this afternoon and asked if he wanted to see a video. I didn't have his phone number, so I looked it up in the telephone book, an act of bravery and momentum. This is the first time I'm seeing him after dark. His old stone house looks different in the evening, a little creepier, but inside it's lit up and cozy. My old copy of *Harold and Maude* is in my book bag. I'm nervous, wondering if this is too crude a courtship move to bring him a film about an old woman and a young guy falling in love. What do I want from him anyway?

At the door, Hal looks happy to see me. He takes me to the kitchen. There are bowls of popcorn sprinkled with parmesan cheese and brewer's yeast. There's also Cherry Coke, which I told him I like but he thinks is awful, so I know that he got it especially for me. It is tantalizing that he bought something for me that in his mind basically equals Satan. We sit on a comfortable tweed couch in the family room, which is filled with pieces of his life: a picture of his wife looking very young and pretty and another of her looking old and not quite as pretty, drawings his kids made, group portraits of his whole family with the grandchildren, shelves of books, and some landscape paintings that his wife made. I usually don't like landscapes because they're all old ideas—usually barns around here or fields, but these seem kind of weird and interesting. One is of a lake in the middle of the mountains with a woman in a boat rowing across, except the rowboat isn't in perspective; it looks wobbly, and half of it is going in another direction, like maybe the painter was trying to show that the woman was changing course. The other is of a stream in the middle of a forest with lush ferns and lots of light and, in the shadows, a cross-eyed lion. They are not very good, but not very bad. I wonder what Jung would say about them, and if Hal's wife felt like she was the woman in the rowboat—alone, and maybe lonely in some deep way, some way that you can still be when you have a husband and children.

I can't believe Hal has never seen *Harold and Maude*, but he hasn't, and I look at him from time to time to see his reaction. Soon he is laughing, and I take a breath and sink into my seat. It makes me feel like a child again being in the family room, watching a movie, eating homemade popcorn with all of the photos of children and people smiling.

Hal seems to really like the movie, and I get swept up in it again. There is a fire in the fireplace, and from time to time, Hal gets up and pokes it with a rod. My feet are up on his wife's stool, and I feel like I could almost fall asleep. The movie, along with the Cherry Coke, brings me up in a slight high. I'm pulled into a bittersweet mixture of sadness and happiness, with the Cat Stevens music giving me a sense of just being in the moment and living before you die. Both of the characters are obsessed with death: Harold, the young man who pretends to kill himself in front of his mother in so many ways—hanging, hara-kiri, immolation, slitting his wrists—and Maude, the seventy-nine-year-old who goes to funerals for fun and lives a totally spontaneous, in-the-moment life. Who am I in this story? Why am I showing this to Hal? Is this some odd thing to be doing? Will it be too close to home for him with the real death at the end? Will it make him sad thinking about his wife?

I look at Hal in the firelight. I don't have a strong feeling of animal attraction like in the sterotype of a movie date, where your hands barely touch and then move away from each other's in shock, but he looks cute there wearing a brown sweater and smiling, his gray hair amazingly thick for his age and the wrinkles around his eyes the kind that come from smiling and laughing.

I pay more attention this time to the love scenes between Harold and Maude, how the erotic tension builds. Harold catches Maude modeling nude for an old painter, and she later asks him if he disapproves. He thinks a minute and says no, and then she asks him, in the voice of a coy little girl, if he thinks it's wrong. She still has a bit of the seductress left in her. The story is rolling around in my head with its theme of how to live before we die, and I start thinking of all of the things I should be doing—traveling or having wild adventures. I should be jumping a box-car right now or having an affair with an Italian soldier or doing strange drugs. Now, this very moment.

Hal is engrossed in the movie. He doesn't know yet that Maude will die. Will he kiss me?

When the movie is nearing the end, my body tightens with tension. Is it because I hate the ending or because I'm afraid of what might happen with Hal after, when we figure out whether this is a date or not? I can't stand to see Harold when he finds out Maude has taken the capsules. When he tells her that he loves her, she says "That's wonderful. Go and love some more." It never really makes sense to me. I guess she wants to die while she is still happy, but I hate her death scene. Harold rushes her to the hospital, and she says he shouldn't be making such a fuss, and then she dies anyway, even though he tried to save her.

I look at Hal's face. I can see the young man in him. His emotions are not far under the surface—hurt, confusion, wanting life to never end. Hal is sitting close to me, but we are not touching. If I moved my arm a bit, it would brush his.

"That was great," he says when the credits start rolling. "I'm a sucker for strange intellectual love stories. The ending was really bittersweet."

"How did you feel when Maude died?" I ask. "I mean, did you think she would die?"

"Well, I guess it fit with the whole theme of the movie about really living and then letting life go, but she still seemed to be having so much fun. Maybe she could have waited until ninety."

"Or at least spent a year with Harold. I've never been able to figure out why she couldn't live a little longer."

Hal smiles and nods. "Yeah, she could have given the kid a year. But for the plot of the movie, it was perfect."

"That's always true, isn't it? You want unhappy stories to end happier, but when they do it ruins the movie." There is a part of me that still wants every movie to end happily. The part that does not like art movies.

"It made me want to go out and do outrageous things," Hal says.

"That's exactly the way I always feel after I see the movie," I say. "What do you want to do?"

"You name it. Let's steal trees or go and liberate something at the zoo." Hal is turned toward me. He smiles when he says this. We are very close. I try to think how the space between us could be bridged. Here I am talking about outrageous things and afraid of crossing these few inches.

"I don't think there is a zoo nearby," I say, "except the petting zoo at the amusement park. You want to liberate goats?"

He laughs. "Well, you're the young one. What do you want to do?"

I think about him touching me. I think about kissing in the park. I think about floating down the river in a boat and ending up in another town.

And then I blurt it out. "Do you ever think of me . . . like a woman?" I feel my ears burning.

Though he smiles, he seems a bit shy. "I can see you're a woman, Claudia." His voice has changed, a little more serious and reserved. He looks like he might be blushing. "A very beautiful young woman."

"So do you ever think of me like that?" I feel slightly dizzy talking this way, afraid he'll laugh at me because I'm a child.

"Well, I guess I do, but I know that I'm way too old for you." He meets my eyes with a sad look. I think about the movie, about how age is meaningless, about how we really only have this moment.

"Maybe you're not. Maybe age doesn't matter."

He laughs. "Like Harold and Maude."

I take a quick breath. Maybe I have been too obvious. Maybe he *is* laughing at me.

"Yes. Was it stupid to bring that movie?"

"No, I loved it. You know, during the movie I was thinking even though you're young, you're a lot like Maude."

"Me? But I'm scared of everything."

"Not really. It's kind of a ruse. I think that you are really fearless under it all. Like here, now, asking if I think of you as a woman." The sadness is gone from Hal's face, and he looks animated, younger.

"It's just a question, and I have to admit I prepared. It wasn't spontaneous."

"It's a brave question, and frankly I don't feel so safe answering it."

I see the blue of his eyes, and then he glances at the fire. He gets up to poke it. Why do people always poke fires instead of talking?

"It's good to not be safe," I say.

"Yes, I guess I usually feel pretty comfortable. Most roads are ones I've been down before. But this is a little different."

He sits next to me again, this time a little bit closer. He slides his hand across the couch and puts it on mine. He rubs his fingers along the top of my hand, and I feel an electric surge to my head and into my pussy. (Would he use that word? How would he describe that part of a woman's body?) He is touching me and looking into my eyes. His eyes are like a cat's, I think, a blue so bright and clear that they have a tremendous ability to reflect everything—a lake, I think, maybe the lake in the painting. I have a sense of myriad things floating inside of them.

"You should go, Claudia," he says, but he is still looking into my eyes.

"Okay, I really liked it here." I lean in a bit. He is moving his lips a little.

"I liked it too." He ducks his head and kisses me on the mouth. His lips feels dry to me and awkward. It's a kiss of another generation, a short peck. I'm not sure I like it, but his hand, his hand still touching my hand, and the idea of his hand touching wherever he wants, that I like.

Outside, the leaves have fallen from the trees and been raked into piles by all the good citizens of Riverton. Next door there is a huge pile of them. Passing, I do what I haven't done in years: I jump into the pile of leaves that Hal's neighbor has raked. I think about going inside and getting Hal and jumping in the pile with him, but he might disapprove. He might think it's too much, and then I would have to be disappointed in him and ruin the night. There are the movies and then there are your neighbors. I lie in the pile of leaves. The moon is full—the pregnant belly look. I see lots of stars. There are beings out there in space who fall in love and get confused and don't know what they are feeling, and then there is one here in a small part of the planet, feeling amazingly free. I shake the leaves off and walk home.

# LUKE

I have been observing Luke in the week since he started temping. We haven't talked, but I like the way he does things. He always smiles and nods when he's given an assignment, but there is a vacant "I'm thinking of other things" look in his eyes that I recognize. He seems like he might actually be alive. I saw him reading Kierkegaard in the break room, and I think that he must be just out of college or starting college, and that's cool. Nobody at work talks about ideas. We are a non-ideas, homey recipes, kid-friendly office. In the break room there is a refrigerator and a coffee can to put money in for the coffee club. The break room invariably smells like cheap flavored coffees: hazelnut, caramel, or vanilla. If you are member of the "club" you are supposed to put money in whenever you drink coffee, and then someone from the club is assigned to buy the coffee each week with the money from the can.

I used to belong to the coffee club, but I found that I always forgot to bring money, or when it was my turn to buy the coffee I would forget to buy it and then there would be a feeling of pressure and disappointment from my coworkers. I found that I couldn't live up to the expectations of the coffee club, so when I want coffee now I take the elevator to the basement, where, in a gray room decorated only with a free calendar from Randy's Auto Service, I can buy the worst coffee in the world for seventy-five cents. I push the buttons that add the terrible fake creamer stuff and sugar. It comes out a grayish-brown color, and the only good things about it are that it contains caffeine and is fairly hot. And that the machine never gives me dirty looks for forgetting the coffee money.

The break room is decorated with notes about state minimum wage and a bulletin board that reads Our Extended Family in big red letters where people post pictures when they have a new baby. Which seems innocent enough, but then sometimes something bad happens, like when Stella Morey lost her baby and then didn't come back with a picture. I felt bad about that and almost wanted to take the board down so she wouldn't have to look at photo after photo of smiling babies, their flesh so obvious, their cheeks so prominent, their hefty baby fatness like small sumo wrestlers. After the pictures go up, everyone coos over them. Today Luke is sitting in the break room, and a woman is looking at the newest baby. He is drinking coffee from the coffee club, but I sincerely doubt he is a member. Luke is wearing a t-shirt that has an alien head on it, a gray alien with the long egg-shaped skull and the big oval eyes. I don't really know if he is making fun of aliens or is interested in them, so I don't ask.

"You're the only one I ever saw read philosophy at this place," I say, sitting next to him with my mutant-gray instant coffee.

"I just do that so my brain doesn't die. It's almost dead." He pretends that he is knocking on his head like an empty shell. He makes a hollow clicking sound with his tongue. "I was studying philosophy in college, but my father thought it was a dead end." He laughs. "Probably right. Enough about death, anyway."

"Yeah," I say, "I probably think about death too much. Tell me about that book."

"Kierkegaard," he says. "He's really into existential choice. Very high fallutin' stuff."

"What's the difference between a regular choice and an existential one?" I ask.

Luke puts aside his worn book, which looks like it was dipped in the bathtub, and I catch the title—*Fear and Trembling*—which sounds ominous.

He starts into a mini-lecture, his voice getting more serious. "Well, Sartre gave the example of a man whose mother is ill, and he has to decide whether to go to war or stay home to care for her. On the one hand, he should go because of obligation to the state, but he should also stay home because of family obligations. No choice is really right, so he must choose out of his own existence."

He raises his voice when he is talking and sounds a little like a preacher when he says *choose out of his own existence*. He looks at me as if asking me to make the choice. His eyes are getting bigger, and he is fidgeting his leg.

"I think all war is wrong." I say, then immediately think it was a stupid comment. That's not what he means. Am I still trying to be dumb so people like me?

"Yes, but that's not the point. This was World War Two, and that was a more justified war. Anyway, the point is that man cannot choose according to external rules. He must choose from outside of society. Kierkegaard is really into the choice that Abraham makes when he goes to the mountain to sacrifice his son. God tells him to take a knife and his son up to the mountaintop to slit his son's throat. Can you imagine? He's going for it, gonna cut his son's throat for God. Whatcha think of that?"

The woman who has been admiring the baby pictures looks at us and then leaves. I have never had a conversation like this at work, about philosophy. It feels almost subversive, and it makes me happy.

"I think you just freaked that lady out. They take the Bible pretty seriously around here."

"Hey, it's their Bible, not mine. If they don't like what's really in there, maybe they should become atheists or something."

He smiles quickly, a little devilishly, and then looks at me straight in the eyes, unnerving me a bit. He has pretty brown eyes and a nice face, open and friendly.

"Do you know a lot about the Bible?"

"Yeah, my parents are Evangelicals. We read the Bible all of the time. It's always floating somewhere in my head, even though I think most of it is BS. I don't live according to it. That's why I read stuff like this."

"Did you grow up here?"

"We moved here from Kentucky. We had even more religion there. Speaking in tongues, that kind of thing."

"What does Kierkegaard think of the story? Are we supposed to kill our sons for God or not?"

"Yeah, at the last minute God is like—psych—you don't need to kill him." Luke is laughing thinking about it.

"Why would God ask him to do something so obviously messed up?"

"It is weird," Luke says, his voice excited. "It's so unlike what we expect from God, and yet it's in the Bible. That's why Kierkegaard is talking about it. Abraham had to step outside of all of the ethics of the day and make this choice. He had to go with faith and with God and not with what society said was right. That's the difference between the real man of God and the man of the church. It means that what they say in the church might not always be the will of God, and you can only know it for yourself, even if it seems strange and wrong."

"Yeah, but what if people are wrong about what the word of God is? You have people like Manson or whoever thinking they know the word of God and killing people."

"Yeah, it's complicated. It's not so black and white, and that's the nature of choice, but my parents see it differently. Every word in the Bible is real."

Luke gives me a deep and knowing glance, like he's just summarized something that is at the very heart of the moment, and it seems like maybe he has, because now I am thinking about my life and what my existential choice might be. Maybe I should choose another life totally different from this one, like becoming a nun or moving to China.

"And what is the existential choice you need to make?" I ask him.

"I dunno," he says. "It's not about me." Then he blushes and continues, "But here's one I was thinking about. Suppose an alien came to you and told you that the whole planet was going to be destroyed and they were taking you away to be saved. Would you go with them or stay with the planet and die? Like is it worth it to live if everyone you know and everything you love is gone?"

I let out a sigh, thinking of everyone I know being dead while I was on a spaceship, watching at galaxies pass by, or, on the other hand, me waving goodbye to the aliens and waiting for the sun-rolled-into-mushroom-cloud blast. "That question just makes me want to cry," I say.

"Ah," he says, "so it's a good one."

*game five*

# YOU ARE AN ALIEN

It is late at night, and I am lying in my bed singing the Carpenters' "Calling Occupants of Interplanetary Craft." I am throwing my voice out into the dark like a lifeline, looking for a catch. My pillow smells like musty baby powder. I want you to come. I have been wanting an alien to come for a long time, and I've had a feeling for days—a vague longing, an intuition of your arrival. I'd been acting like I was pregnant, or like I think I would act if I were pregnant. I baked; I looked at nature and saw the simplicity and design within it; I thought of what your face would look like. And then today I made Poppin' Fresh buns with cinnamon in your honor—the silver color of the tubes and the way you twist them to bring out the rolls always reminding me of a spaceship opening. I have been looking for you, looking for you for months in the normal passageways between dimensions.

*In your mind you have capacities, you know*
*To telepath messages through the vast unknown*
*Please close your eyes and concentrate*
*With every thought you think*
*Upon the recitation we're about to sing*

*Calling occupants of interplanetary craft*
*Calling occupants of interplanetary, most extraordinary craft*

*You've been observing our earth*
*And we'd like to make contact with you*

I want my body to be open like a good spoon.

I think about Elizabeth Klarer. I read a book about her. She was a meteorologist in South Africa who claimed that she was taken to another planet and had a child with an alien scientist named Akon. Why are alien abductees always so convincing? She was madly in love with him and wrote in her memoir, "I surrendered in ecstasy to the magic of his love making." I think about those words over and over, "magic of his love making." I am a little jealous of her. I want to surrender in ecstasy. Akon said that he had been watching her all of her life and waiting for the right time to meet her. Later, she had to leave the planet of Meton because her heart couldn't adjust to the vibrations of the magnetic field, but those things happen in love; difficulties arise.

I glance again at the checklist that I found in a book called *Alien Abduction Instruction*.

1. Be ready for anything.
2. Dress in white.
3. Go to the field, the one you've been thinking about.
4. Don't even consider telling the press. It is hard to be called crazy. It's worse to be institutionalized.
5. Don't worry, be happy.

The last one makes me wonder. Who writes these books? Formerly abducted fraternity boys? They might as well say, *It's all good*.

When faced with alien contact, don't panic. Alien contact has been happening on many levels for the past fifty years. There are studies that say up to 50,000 people have received contact from aliens. Yet it is still not accepted by the mainstream. Don't doubt your experience. Perhaps you have been feeling out of sorts recently, having headaches, strange dreams, hives, or dizziness. These are common precursors of alien contact. Your body is readying itself. Eat a good meal and dress well before abduction. You may be gone for a long time, and alien food does not always match well with our systems. Do not fear, though. Aliens will not allow any harm to come to you. You may become hungry, but would never starve.

Somehow I know that tonight is the night you are coming, and I know where to go. There is a field I have been thinking about for a long time. A field behind an abandoned house, near an old soapstone quarry. A beaver has moved into the old quarry, and I go there sometimes to watch its progress damming up the streams that feed into it. I go at dusk, when the veil between the worlds opens up.

Tonight, I lie on a Mexican wool blanket, gazing at the sky, and then comes the moment abductees have a hard time describing. As I am looking at the clouds, which are lazy and rolling, one of the clouds starts to get bigger and bigger. For a moment it looks like a giant balloon, then it starts to roll open as if it were bursting, like a flower blossoming, and inside it is a silver ship. I know that I have a choice to either lie there or to let my body (or my soul, or what feels like me) rise up into the ship. I think, *Yes, this is what I want.* Then I am inside.

I immediately notice the walls have the softness and color of a rose petal. I wonder if everything looks sort of like flowers in the ship or if this is my own special version of alien reality and everyone sees things differently. Then I see you. You are standing there, and you are the only one. Your body is yellowish but also translucent, so I can see a purplish gel inside of you, moving around; you have no legs but a trunk with a floating mobility. Instead of a head is a hoodlike area, and instead of eyes there are five light holes of different sizes and shapes and five silver octopuslike tentacles. I'm not sure what I like about you, but I do like you. It feels like a childhood crush, making me slightly giddy with a swirling sensation in my chest and face, and my eyes relax. I realize I am smiling.

You are all business at the start. You tell me that you are going to ask me some questions about my life, and I should answer honestly. I feel slightly betrayed by your formality. I wish we could just sit quietly and gaze at each other.

You are holding a stack of my papers. Somehow you got them from my bedroom. You open my journal to a particularly embarrassing section about a boy I liked who didn't like me that reveals how crazy I felt and how I couldn't stand it anymore.

"Tell me about this," you say to me.

I'm confused. "Oh, that's just my journal," I say. "I was just writing how I felt. It's personal."

"We want to understand personal," you say. "We have many records of all of the newspapers and television shows, but we are trying to investigate the personal writing of humans. Why do you write these things? Who are they for?"

I feel silly. I try to remember what I wrote about how cute this boy was and how he had hurt me. It just doesn't seem of intergalactic importance. "I just wanted to express it. Get it out there," I say.

"Is this part of the love ritual?" you ask.

Love ritual. *Love ritual?* I don't know what you are talking about. "What love ritual?" I say. *Would you just have sex with me?* I think. Why are you asking me these questions?

"In the book you write"—and now you are reading my journal—"*Love will never work for me. I try too hard.* How can you try too hard?" you ask.

You are humiliating me without knowing it. Like all humiliation, it excites me a little. I feel exposed but seen.

I don't know why you want to talk about my journal. I thought this would be just sex and fluid sampling, but you are taking your job too seriously. Pointing to the pages written in the large, scraggly handwriting of the severely emotionally disturbed, you ask, "What does pathetic feel like? Here you wrote, *I am pathetic in my love. Pathetic.*" And then, finding a part in my poison journal, you ask, "Why do you write so much about poison? What does it mean? Is botulism a large killer on your planet?"

I start crying. Maybe I cry because I don't know what to say, or maybe because you are calling me on my neurosis, or maybe because, though I am very comfortable with the idea of being abducted by aliens, actually being abducted is a little strange and frightening. You respond to my tears, either because you have been taught that they are a bad sign or because you are not so unlike me. I will never know. There are so many things I will never know, which makes you interesting to me.

"It's okay. Rest," you say like an alien mother. You put me on a surface that feels soft with a complicated texture, like a giant pincushion flower. You let me sleep for some time. Finally, when you wake me up, you say that now you are going to ask me a series of questions that are not personal. Questions about Earth and human life.

I feel like I'm answering questions in school—making things up, lying a little. I feel at a loss to answer them, incomplete in my knowledge. Have I really lived on Earth?

You ask, "What is the relationship between the nation-state called the United States and the much smaller one called Japan?"

Jesus. "I don't know," I say, because I don't know. You could get a better answer somewhere else, from someone who's not just an average citizen. I think of how the aliens are doing field research on me, like anthropologists. How the anthropologist searches out someone to be an informant, to tell them about a culture. But I am the wrong informant. "Can't you get the answer from a book?" I ask.

"Assimilating all of the information that comes to us from textbooks and television is challenging," you say stiffly. "There is much contradictory information."

I think of all of you with your books and television shows and no teacher. It must be overwhelming. You're kind of like seven-year-old kids lost in the woods with a map, but not knowing how to read it. I want to take your alien body in my hands and stroke it. I want you to be, not some generic alien, but real to me. I don't like you worrying so much about information. I don't like you wanting to find the right answer for things. I think that you are smarter than we are, and I hope that you know that.

"You have to learn who to trust," I say.

You seem to take this as a cue. Out of nowhere you say, "What do you think about when you are performing the reproductive act?"

I perk up. This is the kind of question I've been waiting for. I can answer this. I look at you in your holes. "I have fantasies, or I think about love or just the feeling in my body," I say.

"Why does the reproductive act appear so much in films and books?"

I laugh. "That's tough," I say. "Well, there's Freud's answer. He said that sex was the fundamental drive underneath every action. You should read Freud. He's important."

"What do you think?" you ask.

"Well, it's kind of addictive. And it's connected to love and . . . it's fun."

Are you coming on to me? I wonder. Yes, you are. You tell me (shyly?) that you are supposed to learn about sex . . . from acting it out with me. This is an awkward pickup line, but I don't care. I want to see if you have any special energy tricks, some kind of cosmic hoodoo voodoo that will open up my body in a new way. I don't know what gender you are or what kind of sexuality you have. Does it matter? I don't suppose you have a penis or vagina, so I don't guess it does matter, if you even have a gender. I realize that up till now I have been thinking of you as a he because you somehow remind me a little of a boy I knew once from school.

You float toward me and put a cool, long tentacle on my arm. You are moving it up and down along my inner arm, and it has the slight zing of an electric charge. It feels like my arm is becoming lighter and lighter, and I wonder if you are actually doing something to the particles of my body. Will this have lasting effects? Then you move another tentacle (this one hot) along my upper lip, and I feel a smooth pressure against my mouth, not sticky, but with some texture, like a warm strawberry. I don't know what to do, and I don't care. This hot and cold stuff is intriguing. Is each tentacle a different sensation? I look at the light holes in your hood. They are changing to a violet color.

"We will follow the directions in the book," you say.

"Okay," I say. What book? The alien-human *Kama Sutra*?

Your complete awkwardness makes me want to help you. It is as if you are a virgin, but more than a virgin. Not an awkward teenager, but rather like someone skilled in one area who is learning something entirely new. Beginner's mind. I guess we follow the directions in the book. Whatever book it is. I like the comments about following directions. I am lying on the metal table, and you are standing next to me.

"Would you like kissing?" you ask.

"Yes," I say. I am so easy. You put a cold tentacle on my mouth, and this one tastes interesting and sweet, like jasmine. I start licking it.

"You'll have to excuse me," you say. "I don't have a penis."

"Oh, of course," I say.

"I am nonetheless interested in female sexual response," you say.

"That's good," I mumble, thinking I can already see that. I want you to touch me in whatever ways possible. I realize nobody will ever have to know about this. I won't have to tell anyone. I don't want to be on the cover of *National Enquirer* and *Star*—all those stories of crazy women. It's like you and I are the only ones who exist in my world.

I say, "You can touch me and make me orgasm." It's such a strange word, but I don't know if you'll know the word *come*. Then I reason you must have done your research. You probably have Susie Bright in your back pocket. And you do touch me, and I touch you, or something of you, in the way that I have always touched people, feeling my way toward what I think you like. Here, in this nonhuman world, knowing less but still thinking I can please you somehow.

I feel like I am fainting—swooning—and you are doing things to my body, and not just my body but my thoughts too. Yes, you are connecting to me on some other level, reading my mind, maybe, and I am having all kinds of strange memories from my life (or are they from another life?), not stand-out memories, but moments I didn't even know I still held in my head. I remember the first time I dove into a pool and the feeling of shooting forward and the vulnerability of realizing I could hit my head against the bottom, getting out and feeling cold and my Snoopy bathing suit feeling tight and the lifeguard looking at me strangely. What's going on? It's like I've been taken over by a swarm of old memories.

Afterward, I think it wasn't like sex at all, more like a strange interaction I've never experienced. It wasn't conventionally erotic. You didn't bite me or tie me up or say dirty things to me. You didn't look into my eyes and melt with me or tell me you loved me. Yet I enjoyed it immensely. That's the thing about enjoyment. The parts of life you think are going to be so enjoyable, like birthdays and romantic trips, are often horrible, and the things that sound horrible, like really, really awkward sex, can be wonderful.

After you leave, I pine for you the way I pined for an out-of-town boy in high school—the separation between us making us yearn. Where does longing appear in the body? In the hands, the chest, the eyes, sometimes in the throat—a vague desire to make syllables for the other, a need to talk, to communicate, that is cut off. A longing that reaches up into space and finds itself in some distant galaxy. I don't know where you go, and I don't know if you will ever come back.

# SAFETY SEAL

Since the movie with Hal, I have been in an odd mood. I feel like I should be happy because we kissed, but instead I'm anxious. It's been a week, and I haven't called Hal or gone to the library. My apartment is painted yellow, and I have a yellow couch, and everything is an attempt to make it seem cheery, but it isn't really. It is sad and lonely, and sometimes at night I have fears that come to the windows and threaten to break in.

It's midnight, and I can't sleep. I hear my downstairs neighbor putting out their garbage. I see a light on across the street at the Elks Lodge. They are getting out late tonight. Old men wearing sports jackets with balding heads and big bellies leave the Elks, laughing and making jokes about their wives. I don't know what they do there. Some arcane mystery left over from another era? I can't sleep, and my heart is beating strangely. I have a slight heart flutter that nobody seems to believe I have, but at night I often feel it, the rapid and irregular thumping.

For dinner I made a salad that was supposed to include artichoke hearts, but when I opened the jar, I didn't hear it make the popping noise. The popping noise is important to me, and because I wasn't sure if the jar was sealed right, I didn't put them on the salad. Later, thinking I was crazy, I got them out of the refrigerator and ate one. Surely that wouldn't hurt me, and it's stupid to always throw food out, really wasteful, but now I am wondering if I have poisoned myself. Was the jar supposed to pop when I opened it? Did it pop and I just wasn't listening? Because I don't hear the pop, I don't know if it's safe. The existence of the safety seal now make me feel less safe than I would otherwise. Without a safety seal, I would just assume the jar was safely sealed and let it go. The seal means there must be some doubt in their minds as to whether jars are sealed tightly, or they wouldn't have the seal. Will it poison me? Can I get botulism if it has vinegar in it? Does botulism exist only in canned foods? Does food that comes from China or India or Mexico have the same safety standards? Food safety seems like an abyss of possible mistakes. I don't believe that all of the people who are working in the restaurants and all of the people who are working in the processing plants are thinking hard all of the time about everything that could possibly happen.

# THE CLOSET

Tonight, after work, I crawled into the closet. I sat on the shoes with my dresses falling down over my head. I shut the door, and I felt safe in there.

I used to lock myself into my bedroom, but my father didn't like it and took the lock off the door, so I started hiding in my closet. In my memory I crawl in and put all of my shoes and piles of my clothes in front of the door, blocking the entrance, so my father can't get in. I am eight. My closet is filled with books, papers, old plastic bags, dolls, stuffed animals, crayons, art projects from school, a banana I forgot about that became an art object all on its own, small and black and withered, like a decomposing body. I think in another world someone would worship that banana because it's the soul of something, but here it's trash. If my father finds it, he'll say I'm disgusting. I hate to throw anything away. I saw a TV special about dumps and how the things you throw away last for hundreds or thousands of years, just sitting there and making toxic brews.

It is dark in the closet, with the dresses hanging down, brushing my face, causing a slight pleasure and irritation. The thin light gleaming under the door seems to be a beacon from far off, like distant fires. Maybe I am also living in another world parallel to this one. Maybe I slipped into this world from that one. Or maybe if someone opens the closet door right now, I won't really be here at all.

"Is Claudia in the closet again?" my father asks my mom. The wall is thin between the closet and their room, and I can hear them clearly.

"Probably," my mother says. Her voice is lower, and I have to strain a little to catch it.

"What is she doing in there?" My father sounds annoyed.

"She's okay," my mother says.

"There's something not right with her. She needs to be with other kids."

"Oh, Jessie, leave her be. I read that it's okay for kids to have a strong imagination," my mother says.

"You read?" His voice goes up on the word *read*, as if reading were the strangest thing in the world. I can tell he is making fun of my mother, and I don't like it. It makes me angry. "Is that what they are looking for at work, strong imaginations?"

"She's eight. She's not working."

"She's setting down patterns for life."

"I don't really think she is hurting anything. Do you?" my mom asks, more tentative. She doesn't want to make my father mad.

"She should be outside playing games."

I don't want to play games. Kids play with balls and kick them and throw them at each other. Why? My father thinks I'm a mutant. If I'm not careful, he may lock me up, and it won't feel like being in my closet.

# HAL'S WIFE

The dead seem so lonely. I think sometimes about being dead—where we go and what it's like, and do we have hands? I wonder where Hal's wife is now. I've been distracted by thoughts of her since Hal and I kissed. Is she looking down on us, a ghost? Is the world she's in like this one, but without bodies? Does it have her favorite flowers, violets? Even though I didn't know her, I try to imagine what she would think if she saw Hal with me. She might be shocked, or maybe she would smile, or maybe she's in the heaven space, where she doesn't care that her husband kissed such a young woman. I think about death more than most people. Whether it's cold. Whether it's a real place, or one where nothing takes up any space. And if it's not real, what kind of a place is that?

This morning I invited Hal to go for a walk with me. He is sitting outside the library when I get there. It's getting colder now, and he's wearing a wool sweater and a jacket. He looks regal and patrician, like he should live in New England. He is sitting next to the statue of the town founder, who has a duck under his arm for some reason nobody has ever understood. Some story about when he first came to Riverton, and he had a duck. I am wearing my orange cap that makes me feel like I have a purpose.

We walk through town, toward the place where the old coal power plant used to be, a large ruin of a place that is technically private property. Hal reaches out as if he's going to take my hand and then pulls back. I shove my hands in my pockets. The old plant is surrounded by a barbed-wire fence, but large holes have been cut in it. Hal holds the wire up, and I sneak through, and then I hold it for him, and he seems slow as he maneuvers, his shoulder getting caught for a second and then dipping lower, and I am reminded he is not a young man.

Everyone comes here, even though it's off limits. Kids come on their dirt bikes to play around without anyone looking. Young couples come to have sex on sleeping bags or blankets. I come here because I like the cattails that grow in the boggy areas and the trees on the edge of the property, whose leaves at this moment are starting to turn orange and yellow.

After a long silence, Hal says, "What's on your mind, Claudia? You're so quiet. Are you upset that we kissed?"

"No," I say. "Not really. I don't think so, but I've been thinking a lot about death."

"A good thing to think about," he says. We are watching some black birds picking at the grass, maybe looking for worms or seeds. They seem like a symbol of something else. Some days everything seems like a symbol of something else.

"You think so?" I glance at him to see if he is teasing, but he looks serious.

"Why not?" he says. "It's not so horrible when you look at it."

"Aren't you afraid?" I ask.

"No," he says. "What are you afraid of?"

"I have these fears of poisoning myself. I get afraid to eat things. Then I'm afraid I might be crazy for having these thoughts."

The old power building looks a little like an industrial castle. It's been shut down since they built the nuclear plant. There is one large smokestack my mother said used to spew smoke so thick that when she played in the yard at her childhood home, a few blocks away, she would get dust in her hair.

"You have a lot going on in that mind of yours."

Hal puts his hand on my forehead as if I have a fever. There are some old tree stumps nearby, and we sit down. Hal looks kind of old in the gray day. I notice hairs in his ears, which are wiry and curly. I wonder if his wife used to trim them.

"I was troubled too when I was your age," he says.

He was going to law school and then being a lawyer, so how troubled could he have been?

"I've also been thinking a lot about your wife," I say, the words coming out in a sigh.

"That's two of us," he says. He is looking at the sky, the big clouds that could be any shape of your imagination.

"I've been a little worried that she might be watching us from somewhere and feel jealous. Sometimes I picture her—I don't know where this came from, maybe some old TV show—but she has a rolling pin in her hand and is shaking it at us. Other times I think she has just become a cloud and couldn't worry less about it."

"She hated to cook. If she shook anything at us, it would be a gardening trowel and not a rolling pin. I'm for the cloud idea. Sometimes I feel her around me. On the good days. On the bad days she's just gone."

"I don't want to make you feel bad talking about her."

"I like talking about her. People think they will make me feel bad talking about my wife because she's dead, but I would love nothing more than to talk about her for hours. It helps me. I don't think where she is she cares about kissing."

He is looking at a cluster of milkweed pods, the shattered husks with a few strands of milky white silk inside. Two kids about twelve approach us riding dirt bikes. One of them has a stick in his hand and is leaning over and striking anything in his path, small trees growing up, weeds, some old metal cans. He hits a patch of milkweed and sends a plume of white seeds up. The other one is wearing all black and biking fast, head down, in his own world. He makes a sound like he's riding a motorcycle, and then he notices us and stops.

"If it makes you feel better, she told me before she died that she wanted me to date. I laughed because I didn't think anyone would want me." He glances at me, embarrassed. "I didn't mean anything by that," he says. "I don't expect anything from you. How could I? I'm way too old for you."

"I'm sorry I'm so neurotic," I say.

"It's okay. I was the same way at your age," he says, but I don't think Hal ever had all of these weird thoughts flowing through his mind like toxic waste.

"What about the poisoning?" he asks. "What's going on there?"

I see the lawyer in him for a second, working through the objections one by one.

"How do you imagine you poison yourself?" he questions.

"I don't know . . . sauerkraut, botulism, something in the refrigerator that's old, or people feeding me poison food by accident. Does that sound bizarre?"

"Then what happens?" he says.

"I get sick."

"Then what happens?"

"I die."

"Then what happens?"

"I don't know. I don't want to die."

"I'm just saying if the worst happens, then what happens?"

"You're trying to teach me to not be afraid of poisoning by saying I may die, but it would be okay. I'm not sure how reassuring that is." I laugh a little, nervously.

"I guess not. But on the other hand, if all fear is fear of death in some way, then maybe it could help. Are you afraid of death?"

"I think about it a lot."

"I guess my wife taught me all about death. Watching her die was so painful, but I could see in her that she thought it was all right. Even at the end, when she was in such pain from the cancer, she still had moments when she would just enjoy something small like sunlight coming in the window or listening to me read her a story. Always before that, I had been so afraid of death, or maybe not even afraid, mostly not thinking about it, but when I did think of it, then afraid. But I could see that she was okay with it, which struck me as wrong for the longest time. I even felt like she wasn't fighting hard enough, but after a while I realized that couldn't go on forever."

Hal gets up and starts pacing. He is the kind of man who paces when he thinks.

"They say as you get older, you get more and more used to death, but with her, it was different. It was like losing something of me. You have all of these memories that you build together, and you rely on the other person to remember things for you. That's not there anymore. There are lots of things I don't remember. Parts of me that died when she did."

Hal's boots make a cracking noise as he walks on the hard ground. I don't like to hear him talk about this. It's hard to see him upset.

Then he looks at me kindly. "I'm sorry you're afraid of poison. Why do you think you have that fear?"

Is he trying to heal me? Would he be my doctor?

"I don't know," I say. "It starts with a small worry, and then it grows. Maybe I eat some food someone canned at home, in their kitchen, and then I think about how the person might have made a mistake, and how human it is to make a mistake, and if they make a mistake then they could kill me, or I could make a mistake and kill someone."

"So you think about killing other people too?"

"Not really. Not seriously, but I might accidentally. I mean, anyone might, accidentally, at any time. Sometimes when I'm driving I think, what if I hit someone with my car and I don't notice it."

"I wouldn't be afraid of you doing something horrible, and you shouldn't be either. You are a good person. Trust yourself."

The two boys on bikes ride by us again. They have a turtle with them. The one in dark clothes, who looks like a depressive, is holding the turtle, and the other one is saying something about seeing what they can do with it. I'm mildly afraid for the future of the turtle, but the way misfit boy is holding it gives me hope it will become his pet and not their experiment.

*game six*

# DOCTOR

I am the patient, and you are the doctor. You are older and wiser than me, of course; the doctor always is. I keep my body open to you. You analyze my internal organs with special instruments you made to see inside of me. Like little vials, all of my organs line up, emptying and filling with liquids under your gaze.

We invent an extreme form of doctor-patient relationship. In this relationship, the doctor makes love to the patient, psychoanalyzes the patient, and acts out the patient's dreams with the patient.

You are a mime and mimic all of my actions. When I eat curry with cauliflower, you eat curry with cauliflower. When I brush my hair, you brush your hair, even though you don't really have any. It's a form of therapy you came up with called Being The Other. You want me to tell you everything I feel and think, but my thoughts come so fast I can't keep up with them. As I am telling you what I am thinking, I realize I am now thinking something new.

"Who determines if I am healthy or ill?" I ask you.

"I do," you say.

"What if I feel well, but you say I'm sick?"

"Sometimes a disease doesn't show signs until we test, though usually there are decreased abilities."

"Do I have anything?" I ask. "AIDS, cancer, African sleeping sickness?"

"We don't know yet. The tests are unclear. We must continue to test you. In the meantime, I need to know everything you think and feel," you say. "I am getting so very close to knowing exactly what it's like to be you, and then I can cure you."

"Maybe this is wrong," I say. At first I thought if you knew everything about me, it would be a form of love, but now I wonder if you are becoming me. Once that happens, I think you will no longer need me for your experiments. You have funny hairs growing in your ears, the kind of hairs men get when what is inside of their heads starts to come out. Why won't the parts of your body stay inside! The hairs remind me that I am a young woman and you are an old man and therefore you cannot ever truly become me.

# MOM

It's Sunday, late November. It's raining and becoming more gray. Fall is easing into winter, and I find myself falling into small pits of depression, staying inside to hide from the darkness. Maybe I have Seasonal Affective Disorder.

I start to leave my house to visit my mother, but I can't find my keys. Yesterday I looked all day for a letter I remember writing, but I couldn't find it either. My apartment is covered with a layer of papers like autumn leaves. I search through the bedclothes and discover a book I'd been reading a week ago, a novel that Hal recommended, *Housekeeping* by Marilynne Robinson—ironic. I look under my bed, and it's a shameful mess of things I have pushed under there: Kleenex, some old bills, underwear, coins, a pen, a necklace that broke, some color Post-it pads I stole from work, lots of paint strips with the little blocks of color, a stuffed animal goat I sometimes sleep with that my mother gave me when I was five, a book about poison, a stick of gum, and the blueberry lip gloss I wore when I watched the movie with Hal. I imagine Hal's lips on mine, and suddenly this thought fills me with dread, as if I am kissing a man who is already dead. I fear I will keep falling in love with older and older people and then fall in love with the dead. I will slip into the morgue and undress the men, touch their cocks, and make love to them. Under the foot of the bed, I see the pants I was wearing yesterday. My keys are in the pocket.

On Sundays I visit my mom, a habit left over from when I was a kid and we went to grandma's for Sunday dinner, but now grandma is dead and my other relatives have moved to exotic places like Cleveland, so I visit Mom, who still lives in the same ranch house with yellow siding that I was born in. My mother has lived there alone since I moved out. She never remarried, doesn't even date. I think she was tired of the whole thing by the time my father disappeared. When she was young, my mother was very beautiful, and she could have picked anyone, but she picked my father because he made her laugh. I guess he was more amusing when he was younger. I remember he could be funny at times, just not usually. He used to tell me jokes and stories, and some days he would seem like he was in a Broadway musical, everything a song and a dance, but then he would have bad days, days when he was impossible to talk to—days when everything he said was sour and everything we did was wrong. Those days became more and more frequent.

The house is pretty much like it was when I moved out. Mom wanted me to live there forever, but when I was nineteen I decided that I was too old to live with my mother. She tried to convince me I could save money staying with her, but I felt like if I did stay, I would never change. I would always take the garbage out, do the dishes, always argue with my mother about what a nice sweater is or isn't, never have a lover, and never do something so bad I was ashamed of myself. We were too close, I thought, and though I couldn't move to another city and abandon her, I could move across town. She didn't talk to me the day I left. I borrowed a neighbor's pickup truck, and in complete silence she helped me load box after box in the bed.

The house is white with yellow trim, and my mother usually has pansies and impatiens out front in the summer, but today the only thing giving color is the red Chinese maple out front. All around, up and down, are the streets people moved to years ago to have kids, but those kids are grown, and now a lot of older people live here alone. Sometimes they sell the places to young families, and so occasionally I see toddlers and kids in wagons. A few of the kids I grew up with now have kids of their own and live around the corner from or next door to their parents. I remember thinking the other kids in the neighborhood all seemed to belong to some club, and I was not in it. They were all so naturally childlike, and I felt like an old person in a child's body, worrying and being self-conscious.

I let myself into the house with my key. Mom is sitting on the white couch. The white couch is her one symbol that she is not a full-time mother anymore. She always wanted a white couch and bought it after I had grown up. Still, the white couch is getting a little gray. There is a bag of open potato chips at her feet. Bickel's. It seems like she's been crying.

"Hey, Mom. What's wrong?" I sit beside her, and she looks at me blankly.

"I'm too fat," she says.

She tries to stop crying, but tears are still running down her wrinkled but pretty face. I put my arm around her. She feels nice, and I remember as a kid loving her big lap.

"Oh, no, Mom. It's okay." Sometimes I feel a little like I'm propping my mother up, and if I left—like really left—she would fall over.

"I am," she says. "I'm disgusting."

She is wearing polyester pants and a green and blue sweater. She has short curly black hair that is graying, and she could lose maybe fifty pounds, but she still has a pretty face and bright blue eyes that I envy. She looks fat, but nice. I think how her weight doesn't matter, and no way should it make her feel like this.

"It's okay," I say. "You look good to me." She looks the same way she has for twenty years. I don't really think anything is going to change.

"Don't say that. I just can't do anything about it."

"I know," I say. "I'm fat too." I am a little overweight. In good moments, I think of my figure as generous. If she hates herself, then do I have to hate myself too?

"No, you're not," she says. "You're pretty."

"Pretty fat," I say, thinking pretty is not the opposite of fat. "Did something happen?" Usually there is a trigger with mom.

"Oh," she sighs. "Well, yes. . . . I've been on a diet for a month, and I gained a pound. I gained a pound on my diet. I went on it with Ruth Geyer down the block, and Ruth has lost twelve pounds. I tried. I really tried in the beginning, but I've been cheating. She's my diet buddy, and I have to call her and tell her my progress. She wants to talk all the time so she can gloat." My mother has moved from sad to angry. "The phone just rang. I knew it was her, so I didn't even answer. Probably lost another pound."

"The chips," I say. I can't help smiling, because Bickel's are her favorites. At least she didn't fall off the wagon for Pringles.

"Depression," she says. "But I've been mostly good."

"It's hard."

I want to make weight go away. I want my mom to not worry about something so superficial, but I can't. The TV is on in the kitchen, and it gets loud as a commercial for crackers comes on. People so goddamned excited about a piece of baked flour. Of course, this is what we have to swim in. All of it, all the time.

She sighs and looks around. "I'm sick of it," she says. "Sick and tired of being fat and sick of trying."

"Well, nobody cares," I say, "and you're not that fat."

Outside our picture window, the mailman walks by. I notice him and know the one thing that can distract my mother from being fat is the mail.

"Mail's here," I say.

"Oh," she says, and gets up. A cool breeze comes in when she opens the door, and I see the neighbors who walk every day out there walking around and talking. They stand out in this town because nobody else walks anywhere.

Mom comes back looking disappointed.

"Anything?"

"No. A bill. Some catalogs." She throws them down on the coffee table.

My mother and I are eternally hoping that something good will come in the mail, but nothing does. I'm not sure what we think is going to arrive that is so magical. Maybe someone we didn't know we were related to dies and leaves us a mansion, or we win a trip to Greece in some sweepstakes.

My mother feels things too much, and sometimes she lets things get her down. I used to be the one she turned to with her feelings; we had a club between us two. She would tell me what was bothering her. Even before my father disappeared, when everything was building up in a swirl of getting worse and worse and knowing that you're going to drown. That's how it felt before he was gone; there was always this vague foreboding that something bad was going to happen, and for me that was worse than something bad actually happening. She knew that something was wrong, but she didn't want to deal with it. I felt that something was wrong, but I didn't know what it was.

I sympathize with her now. I can't diet. It's hard to lose weight, and it's bad to be fat. The fat cells will eventually take over the world, and somehow we cannot run far enough. I suspect if we had more money we wouldn't be fat. Somehow rich people stay slim. It doesn't really make sense, because you would think that since they can afford to eat whatever they want, like lobster for breakfast and truffles for dinner, they would eat a lot. I guess they all have spas and personal trainers. But here in my life, when things are not what I want them to be, I eat a doughnut. Even though I know better than to care about appearance, and technically I know that women's bodies are something they should be proud of (even at my lame community college we read feminist books, so I know all that stuff about body image and the role of women), I still feel fat. It's like I can't get my mind around it. And she can't either. I've dieted on and off since I was a kid, and there's always this feeling of it not working and not being good enough and then being ugly as punishment. Fat is even worse than ugly, because ugly is something that you don't bring upon yourself. Fat is something you can control. And I feel double guilty for being fat because so many people are hungry. Being fat makes me an ugly American.

Mom sits on the couch reading a catalog that came in the mail. "Look at this pond thing," she says, pointing to an ad.

"What's that?" I ask, leaning toward her. I notice more gray in her hair.

"A do-it-yourself koi pond for a hundred twenty-five dollars. It might be nice to watch the fish swim by. Would you like that?"

"Oh, I think those things just go bad quickly," I say, and as I'm saying it I think, *Why do I have to be so negative?*

"Yeah, I guess you're right," she says, still looking wistfully at the fish.

"But it might be nice to see the fish swim by," I say.

It's the idea of the fish that's important. Maybe the idea can cheer her up. I want her to be happy. I want her to get over her weight. I want her to be better than me.

"We don't have much room for a koi pond anyway," she says, and turns the page of the catalog.

"Do they die in the winter?" I ask.

"Who?" she says, looking up at me.

"The koi," I say, irritated that her attention span is two seconds. "How long do they live?"

"I don't know," she says, still looking at other junk.

"You must have to bring them inside for the winter or something. I couldn't see fish living in the frozen water."

"I guess not," she says.

"Well, I guess we're not getting a koi pond," I say.

Now she's looking at a fountain of a boy peeing, an eternal spring of pee. I don't know who would ever buy that. At least she has forgotten being fat, I think, but then she looks up from the catalog, and her eyes dart to the chips bag, a look of sadness crossing her face.

Sometimes my mother wants things like koi ponds or bread machines, but she doesn't have much extra money, so she talks about these things for a bit and then figures out a reason she doesn't want them. It's a good technique. I have learned this technique too, and I don't know if it's bad because I'm lying to myself or if it's good because I buy less.

After my father disappeared, my mother got a part-time job with Avon, but she was never a good salesperson because she thought people didn't need too much. She tends to wear the same clothes forever. She halfheartedly tried to sell things, and we always had a lot of Avon jewelry because people ordered things they didn't want and she hated sending things back, so she would buy them. Today she is wearing a gold cat pin from Avon. I still have a pin that's a little girl in a blue dress that opens up to a buttery perfume inside. I was thirteen when Mom gave it to me, and it was much too childish for me, but that didn't stop her. I have one of a gingerbread man too.

My mother would go door to door selling and have parties, and sometimes other women who were higher up in the company would come over. The other women were always well put together with a lot of makeup and nice scents. They had nice handbags and shoes, too, and they would leave multicolored lipstick stains on the wine glasses. My mother bought shrimp for them, something she would never do for us. They were small shrimp, and she worked them into appetizers as a way of showing her guests they were special and deserved high-class food. My mother never really liked these women, though. After they left, she would clean up the fancy stuff she had bought especially for them and feed us regular food like Tuna Helper.

My mother was a bad Avon lady, but she was a good friend. She could never tell anyone to stop talking. Women would tell my mother about their children's troubles in school, their husband's affairs, or even their own affairs. She is a good listener, and when she went to the houses to sell Avon or drop it off, she would get into long conversations with the customers, and it often seemed like it wasn't worth the money because she would spend hours on a single order. Though she listened to everyone else's troubles, Mom never talked about herself, or about my father leaving us. That was our secret. I know because she told me not to talk to anyone about it, and when I went with her on house calls, she never said a word.

Once, we left a house after two hours, and the woman only bought a tube of lipstick. I told my mother that she shouldn't talk so long to people who don't buy, but my mother said it was part of her job, that when people buy Avon they buy the personal attention of an Avon lady.

I said, "It's kind of pathetic that they have to buy a friend."

My mother shot me a cold look and told me not to judge. "We have each other," she said, "but not everyone has that."

I remember feeling in that moment both taken care of and trapped. We had each other, but what did that mean? That I could never rely on others, or tell anyone the truth about Dad, for the rest of my life?

"Are you okay, baby? You seem distracted."

I've been staring out the window at the maple tree. Finished with the mail, Mom picks up the remote control and flips through channels until she finds an old movie.

"I guess I am a little distracted." I've been wondering if I should talk to my mom about Hal. Maybe I could disguise who he is. I have a hard time not spilling things to my mother.

"What's wrong?'

"I've been sort of dating." I don't know why I am saying this. I can't tell her about Hal. She would think I was crazy.

"Well, that's good, isn't it? Do you like him?"

"Yes."

"Then what's the problem?" She looks at me. She wants me to tell her what's going on. I used to tell her everything, but this is too weird.

I'm quiet, trying to think of what to say and how. If I really didn't want her to know anything, I wouldn't have brought it up, but I don't want to tell her the truth.

"Well, you don't have to tell me the details if you don't want to, Claudia." Her voice is a little hurt. "He's not married, is he?"

"No, he's not." *Widowed* pops in my head. *Widowed, widowed.* I tuck that word in a box that I keep for such things.

"Does he make you happy? That's the most important thing."

My mother always has simple answers like this. It makes me breathe a little easier, though, to think that it just comes down to being happy or not happy. The problem is I don't know if I'm happy or not.

I ask myself, *Does Hal make me happy?* He makes me think about myself in a different way. He makes me wonder at my fears instead of being quite so caught in them. When I'm with him I feel a little more space in the world to be myself. Is that love?

# POISON DIARY: NANNIE DOSS

I started the poison notebook after I read a book about Love Canal—
about all of the children getting sick because their town was built on
toxic waste. I always had the idea that something terrible would happen
here in Riverton, and a cloud of dust would hang over us, and we would
all be dead. Maybe we were already dying from the poisons in the food
and in the air. When I read about Love Canal, I thought I would surely
uncover something like that in my town. I don't remember the exact
day I started keeping the poison notebook, but I know I was thirteen,
reading the book about Love Canal, when my mother came into the
room. I was lying on the bed with a copy of *Seventeen* magazine and the
book. She asked what I was doing, and I told her I was trying to figure
out what was real. Yes, I wanted to wear the hot new colors and have
hair that was bouncy and pretty, but I also didn't want to die of unknown
chemicals—not in dyes or perms or in barrels under the city.

At Love Canal, they kept seeing the numbers of children with cancer
increasing, and they found out there were pits of chemicals—a slush of
toxic waste—buried under where they built the school and playground.
The dirt the children would play on was made of dioxins and benzene
that had seeped up through the soil. I started the poisoning notebook to
take note of these things.

In my poison notebook I record famous instances of poisoning, news
accounts of poisoning, and ideas about foods I've eaten that might kill
me. I tuck in articles I've clipped—about women poisoning their husbands, or corporations poisoning towns, and everyone, everywhere, with
some poison in their bodies. Breast milk is contaminated by things in

the environment, for example, and babies are drinking pesticides right from their mothers.

Maybe I am disturbed. Maybe I should concentrate on something healing. But I'm intrigued with the mind of the poisoner, someone who chooses to put death into another's body. I wonder what makes a poisoner different from someone who strangles or shoots someone. Poisoning seems to have a mental component that is absent from other murders. I think because it's a secret. You can poison someone without them knowing. When you pull a gun and shoot someone, the hatred and the harm are out in the open, but poisoning is murder plus a lie.

If you are going to kill someone, poisoning seems like the most intimate and stealthy means—an act of murder in which you never need to directly confront the victim, and yet you enter the victim, or your concoction does. It is so feminine in the way it enters the body, a secret that will work against it.

Statistically, women poison more than men do. There are two main reasons for this. First, we have the greatest access to food because it's considered our duty to feed men, and second, it takes no physical strength. Poisoning can succeed even if the victim is much bigger than the poisoner.

Nannie Doss, known as the Giggling Granny, is one of my favorite poisoners. I read about her while sitting in the Riverton library. I looked around and thought that many of the women there in the reading room could have been her—a housewife and a mother, a grandmother. She poisoned most of her family and killed four husbands over twenty-eight years, until she was finally caught in 1954. She fed her victims rat poison, sometimes soaked prunes in it and then baked them in her special prune cake. She started by killing two of her infant children, and went on to kill her second, third, and fourth husbands, along the way killing her mother, a mother-in-law, and two grandchildren. She was a country woman who believed in romance and always read romance magazines. Her husbands, whom she met through lonely hearts letters, always seemed in the letters to be much better than they actually were; she was eternally disappointed.

The part of the story that really hurts my heart is how she killed her one grandson right after he was born. While her daughter was in the hospital, the baby mysteriously died. The daughter, still groggy after giving birth, thought she saw her mother putting a needle into the soft part of the newborn's skull—but it couldn't have been true, she told herself, just a hallucination from the drugs and exhaustion. When the cops caught Nannie, she wouldn't stop reading her romances, and they had to take away her magazines to get her to talk. The press called her the Giggling Granny because she laughed through the whole trial.

# LUNCH WITH LUKE

Luke is a member of a band, but he doesn't play any instruments. His role, he says, is to provide the creative direction for the band and to keep the politics in line. The worst thing a band can do, according to Luke, is to make music that's popular but has no plea for the future of the world and for revolution. A lot of music has become another consumer good, has lost the power to unite people and create an uprising. Luke writes some lyrics and makes sure that the band maintains its connection to the people. I wonder what *connection to the people* means.

Luke and I are at The Gingerbread Man, a restaurant near work, having lunch. I am pretty sure he's gay. If he wasn't gay, I would be in love with him and he would be in love with me. That's what I think, but none of this is ever said, and maybe I'm wrong. In the few months that he's been a temp, we've developed a friendship. We talk in the coffee room and we trade audiobooks that we listen to while we're at work. I'm allowed to listen to the books while I do my data processing, since it doesn't take any mental energy. Luke is allowed to listen when he's not answering phones. We check out audiobooks from the library, but it's hard to find good ones. This week I listened to some self-help thing about loving yourself more and a Stephen King novel. Luke gives me a Shonen Knife album to listen to and The Sugar Cubes.

Luke hates or loves everything. Mostly he hates the government, our town, politics, and temping for our company, which he says is like a black hole eating him up. When I say, "So why don't you leave?" he says he's going to and that's why he is saving money and working at this suck-ass job. He tells me that he's an anarchist, and I don't really know what that is, but I don't comment because he seems to know things.

The Gingerbread Man is known for their Buffalo wings dipped in blue cheese dressing. It has some mirrors on the walls and ferns and is painted green and white. It's all very unoriginal. I order a chicken sandwich. Everything on the menu is rich and fried or dipped in butter or with hollandaise sauce or with ranch sauce or cheese.

Luke orders something called killer fries, which are fries loaded with cheese and sour cream. "I'm a vegetarian," he says. "I can't stand to kill living beings."

"I wish I could be a vegetarian," I say, "but I can't stick with it."

Luke starts playing with the salt and pepper shakers. I've noticed he has a frantic energy. He's making them dance a little.

"I watched one of those movies," he says, "where they show the slaughterhouses. In a way I wish I hadn't watched it. It's terrible. Really ghoulish. The whole *Jungle* thing isn't over."

"Where did you see the film?"

"Some group in Atlanta that I used to belong to. They were sort of political. Showed films about the Contra wars and Reagan. You don't get shit like that here."

"Yeah, people here are pretty apolitical."

He sighs and looks kind of defeated. "It's not so good. I try not to hate them because hatred only leads to violence, but they are so strange. Instead of making decisions in my family, we had to all pray and think on things and ask Jesus what he wanted for us. We get down on our knees together as a family and pray. The sick thing is I still do it, even though I don't believe in it at all. I don't want my father to wither up and die or have a heart attack if I stop. If I told him what I believe, he might just die. I mean, probably not, but still I feel like he really might."

I imagine Luke praying with his family and the feeling of their knees on the floor and how his mother probably keeps the floors very, very clean because they are always down there. I imagine them praying to help him become a better Christian. It is a wholly depressing image. Still, it gives me a degree of sympathy for Luke. Betty from work walks in, and I hope that she doesn't see us, but she does, and she actually comes over to our table.

"Hi," she says. "I didn't know you two were friends." She smiles.

I nod methodically.

"That's so nice," she says.

I redden with embarrassment, but when I look at Luke, he is smiling at Betty like a choirboy. She walks away with a pleasant expression on her face. I wish that I could be nicer to her, but something is physically stopping me.

"What about you? You like it here?" Luke asks.

"Not really, but I guess I'm attached." What am I attached to, I wonder. "I don't think I could leave my mother alone. She would be sad without me. Maybe I don't want to leave, either."

Does that sound strange to him? I wonder if he thinks I'm just a hick and not sophisticated.

"I wish I was two hundred thousand miles from my mother, but she wants me close so she can keep an eye on me, make sure I'm dating girls."

"I guess my mother is a little fragile," I say. It makes her sound like a glass toy. Is she fragile? I think of *The Glass Menagerie.* "What I mean is that when she's sad or depressed, she likes to talk to me. I'm the only one she has since Dad is gone and her parents have passed away and her only sister lives in Cleveland."

My chicken sandwich, no mayo, on a bun looks kind of pathetic. I ask the waitress if she has any jalapeno peppers she could put on it. Anything to help make it a little interesting. She does. I end up doctoring most food in this way, to avoid the gobs of mayonnaise and butter that they put on things. I have a fear of fat that is natural enough, I guess.

When Luke's fries come, they are dripping in cheese and sour cream.

"Those are going to kill you," I comment.

"So the menu says."

"Yes, but they are serious, and that's the evil part of it."

"Well, maybe evil is a strong word. Do we really know what evil is? In *Beyond Good and Evil,* Nietzsche argues that there really is no good or evil. They are concepts that we throw around in different ways and that keep changing."

I like talking about philosophy with Luke, but sometimes it feels like he is using it to avoid telling me about himself—always asking questions and making me debate him. Like he took some philosophy classes in college and is using his knowledge to figure out the whole world, when all I want is to find out more about him.

Our waitress is an overly friendly type who comes to the table continuously to ask if everything is all right.

*No, it's not that good,* I think to tell her, or, *Yes, it's all right, if you mean edible and not as bad as McDonald's.* I don't say either, of course.

"You ever been in love?" Luke asks me out of the blue.

"No, not really, though I might be falling now," I say.

"For me?" He looks me intensely in the eyes, as if he has just fallen in love with me, but I know he's kidding.

"No, not you."

"I'm crushed," he says, smiling. His hands are putting fries quickly into his mouth, and he is licking his fingers with pleasure. He has long fingers and does everything with a slightly theatrical air. He is attractive in a way, but seems incapable of taking anything seriously.

"You are not," I say and eat my healthy food.

"I guess not," he says and puts some fries on my plate. I don't know if he's intuitive or if I unconsciously glanced at his fries with longing.

"Do you even like women?" I ask, then feel embarrassed. I have a habit of speaking without thinking.

"It's up for debate." He shrugs and moves his head to one side and then the other. "I like women," he says. "But not exclusively. Is that okay?" He breathes fast, and I can hear him, as if he is winded and nervous. I imagine his mother down on her knees, praying.

"Yeah," I say. "Sure. I didn't mean to pry."

"S'okay," he says and winks at me. "Do you like women?" he asks.

"No, I don't like women like that." Do I? I don't think so.

I steal a look at a businesswoman at the next table to see if she's eavesdropping, but she and her friend are discussing something in business lingo, saying the words *micromanaging* and *team player* a lot.

"Then why don't you have a boyfriend? Around here, everybody seems to, or a husband, or a dead husband."

"I don't get along so well with everyone." I don't know what to say: that I dream of finding someone all of the time but never do, that I'm in love with an eighty-year-old.

"Yeah, I can see the pickings are slim."

"You think that's the problem?" I take a breath and sigh. It's nice to hear that he thinks the difficulty is the lack of possibilities and not me.

"Well, yeah. You're a reasonably smart girl, and you want more. People here are set in their ways."

"Thanks. Reasonably smart. Nice," I mumble. "The guy I like isn't at the office," I say. My stomach rumbles as I start to talk. If I tell Luke about Hal, he will be the first one who knows my secret.

"High-school sweetheart? Captain of the football team who never noticed little ole you until now?"

"No, he's older."

Now Luke is looking at me with the interest of a cat watching its prey. "Oh, really. I like older too. Mature, experienced. I went out with a thirty-year-old once," he says.

"Yeah, he definitely has experience."

"Is he married?" Luke asks. "I'm not judging."

"Widower," I say quietly, wondering if I'm going to totally alienate Luke if I tell him the truth.

"That must be tough. How did his wife die?"

"A stroke. She was seventy."

"Oh, wow. Why was he married to such an old woman?"

"She was younger than him," I say, watching for his reaction.

He seems to find this humorous. "You are too warped, Claudia," he says, grinning "How old is he? Here I thought I was the deviant one."

"Eighty," I say. Now he is laughing quite a bit. "And what exactly do you find attractive about a decrepit senior citizen? You want his money? Sugar daddy? Should I call you sugar baby?"

"No, it's not like that. He's sweet. I think he understands me. Besides, age is a number, and our souls don't have an age."

"Yeah, okay, but bodies do. Twenty-five-year-old men can be sweet, understanding, *and* hot."

"I know. Maybe it's just my imagination gone wild."

"So you haven't actually done the deed with this guy?"

"Nope. We kissed."

"You like to live in your imagination, don't you?"

"I don't know," I say. "I don't care. I guess I'm looking for love, but what's wrong with that?"

"Nothing. You're idealistic. Once you've had your heart broken a few times, you get over some of that. You probably have romantic ideas of being in love forever. I can tell that you're intellectual and sensitive. When you put those qualities together, you get an overly romantic soul, like Shelley or Keats, some romantic poet. It can be trouble."

"You like making theories about things, don't you? And I'm another one of your theories."

"Maybe, but let me ask you this, do you really think you'll find your fantasy in an eighty-year-old man? I hate to be blunt, but can his hot dog even pop?"

"I don't know," I say. "Maybe. Maybe it doesn't matter."

"It matters," Luke says.

"What about you?" I say.

"I have my options," he says.

"Sure, I spill everything, and then you're all elusive and quiet."

"Maybe I'm seeing someone right now," he whispers, "and his hot dog definitely pops." We both start laughing a little too loud for The Gingerbread Man.

# LOVE?

I have avoided the library for a week. I don't feel like facing Hal, even though he sent me a note on stationery with violets thanking me for the movie and the walk. I'm bleeding, and the blood is moving out of me in big rushes today, and all I really want to do is lie on my bed on a Saturday afternoon and read Anne Sexton poems and think about how awful and wonderful life is. Like her poem, life is an awful rowing toward God. But Anne killed herself, of course, and so I decide to get out of bed and go to the library.

I sludge there, but I go because sometimes I have to act. When I arrive, it's about four o'clock, and I don't see Hal around. Behind the counter, I notice a woman I have never seen before. It's strange, because I know everyone at the library, and I feel a kind of slight shock, a bit affronted that a stranger is behind the desk. I almost want to jump over the counter and take her place. She is thin with long black hair and is maybe in her late twenties. I wonder what she could possibly be doing here. Maybe she's an imposter who just came off the street and is pretending to be a volunteer. Most of the librarians have moles and grandchildren. One I remember, who'd been here in my childhood, was named Puscrum, and she had a giant mole, and I thought that was the name of her mole, so I called moles that for a while. I see the pus and the crumb coming together and a big crash.

This woman is wearing a bright blue shirt and brown slacks. She has shiny hair that hangs below her shoulders and warm brown eyes. She's too young to work here. She's too pretty to work here.

I go up to the counter to ask where Hal is. Maybe he's in the back cataloging new stuff.

"Hi, what can I help you with?" she says, very friendly, but not waitress friendly—professional friendly. She is smiling and looking at me with interest. The way that she is looking at me makes me like her suddenly.

"I come to the library a lot. Are you new here?" I say and smile.

"Yes, I just started yesterday. I moved here from Philadelphia."

She says Philadelphia instead of Philly, although everyone calls it Philly, and I like the fact that she says the full word. It makes me think of what an interesting sounding word it is, and how the first part of it is the Greek root for love, *phil*.

I wonder if I'll feel comfortable checking out books in front of her, and if she'll talk to me about books or if she'll be too cool for me, too professional—if she'll be the kind of librarian who will scowl or the kind who will help your fines magically disappear. She is looking at me like she is really seeing me, with curiosity. I can't imagine her scowling. She might be the rare librarian who really loves books and wants others to love them too.

"My name's Rose Vicente," she says.

"Claudia," I say. Then, "Hecht." My last name always makes me feel a little nervous. There is something slightly sinister about it. I think it sounds like hex, and I'm a witch. We have these traditional Pennsylvania Dutch hex signs that keep away bad spirits, and I always think of them when I say my name.

"So you come here a lot?" she asks.

"Yeah, I guess I'm a regular." I feel a little ashamed that this is what my life consists of.

"It's good to see someone different," she says. "It's mostly high school kids and mothers, and women looking for romance novels." She eyes me like she's sizing me up. "You're not looking for a romance novel, are you?"

"No," I say. "Never could read one of those things. I've always wondered what women see in them. It seems like every one of them is the same page over and over."

We are having a simple conversation, but underneath I feel a small excitement. Maybe she will be my friend. That would be two new friends in a month and would set a record for me.

"What do you like to read?" she asks.

"Novels, health stuff, poetry, some psychology," I say, thinking *weird books on poisoning*. I can't reveal too much of myself at once. I might scare her off. "What made you move here?" I ask, thinking Philadelphia is a lot more interesting than Riverton. What would make anyone move here? Maybe she is running from an abusive boyfriend and seeking shelter here, or maybe she got so many parking tickets that she had to leave town or go to jail.

"It's hard to get a good librarian job. They had an opening here for someone full time, so I applied. I guess I wanted to move somewhere I could afford to buy a house." She smiles at me again, as though she likes me.

She is wearing no makeup. Her face is square, and she has high cheekbones and olive skin. She looks part Asian. Her eyes are brown with maybe some flecks in them. I can't stare at her eyes right now. It's impossible. I look away. She makes me feel awkward somehow, and I don't know if it's because she's from the city and her life is more exciting than mine, or if it's something else.

"Will you stay here a while?" I ask. Then I think there was something wrong with that question. Maybe it sounded like I wanted her to stay.

"Yeah," she said. "I'm buying a house." She laughs. "It's really kind of amazing. I came here a month ago to interview, and I looked at places, and when I found out I got the job, I put in a bid on this little pink bungalow. They took my offer."

"Wow, that's great," I say. I can't believe someone like her is moving here. She seems much too cool for this place.

"Well, housing here is cheap, and I always wanted to own something. In Philly I had an apartment," she says. "I still can't believe I'm buying a house. I'm signing the papers tomorrow." She seems only a few years older than me, maybe five. They say to look at someone's hands to tell how old they are, so I steal a glance. Her hands are thin and her fingers long. She has very nice fingers. No age is apparent in her hands. I wonder what they smell like.

"That's great," I repeat.

"It's kind of quick and strange. My friend thinks I'm crazy for moving here. Am I?" She laughs a little.

"Well, maybe." I laugh too. "It's not too exciting. Most people who don't have kids want to find a way to move away."

"Well, you seem like a nice person. I'll take this as a good omen. No kids, right?"

"No kids," I say. "I hope I'm nice. People say a place is what you make it. I always thought it was an excuse for people stuck in a place they don't want to be, but maybe it's true."

She looks at me like she is examining something inside of me and trying to figure out who I am. "You're honest," she says. "I like that."

"Well, we should celebrate your new house sometime," I say. The words just slip from my lips, and I know that implies something, that it is a gesture of friendship, but also maybe is too forward. I don't know her.

"Sure," she says. "I'd like that. I need to make some friends."

Suddenly shy, I feel like I have pushed too much, been too open. "Nice meeting you," I say, and turn toward the door.

"I'll see you around soon," she says.

I am conscious that she is looking at me as I'm leaving, and I don't want to do it in a foolish way—turning and looking back, for example, or dropping anything—so I just walk out the door in one motion without stopping at the community board where they post upcoming events, or browsing on the new book shelves like I usually do. I wonder why I am doing everything so self-consciously, why I am so concerned suddenly about how I am moving. When I get outside I realize that I forgot to ask if Hal was there.

# NOTES ON POISONING

To accidentally poison is not evil, but simply the result of human fallibility. We do wrong things without knowing and make mistakes that kill people. There is something strikingly frightening about this to me. Right next to my fear of being poisoned is my fear of causing the death of someone else. Before I worked at the state, I worked as a waitress, and I would sometimes think that I had somehow killed someone without knowing it. One night, after a long shift in which I'd spilled an ice cream cake in someone's lap, I broke some glass near the ice machine. I cleaned it up, but I imagined shards of glass getting into the ice and then into drinks and then customers dying of internal bleeding. At home in bed, I played over the scene again and again in my head. Was I being irresponsible? Should I rush back there and stop everyone from drinking? I was afraid to go into work the next day for fear that they would tell me someone who had eaten there had died, but then I also had a fear that I would never know if someone had died as a result of something I'd done. I would scan the newspapers for stories, worried I would read about someone with an unknown cause of death, or death from internal bleeding, or someone who had died from ingesting glass at the Parkside Diner.

In the process of looking for articles, I came across many stories that scared me. And obituaries. Whenever I read obituaries I think of my mother and feel glad if the dead person is older than she is, as though somehow that gives her more years to live. If the person is younger than my mother, I reason that they were probably a heavy smoker or drinker.

# LADY OF THE RIVER

I go back to the library the next day. I know Hal isn't working, but I want to see Rose again. Last night Rose kept creeping into my thoughts here and there. I wondered what she was like and if we could be friends and thought how she seemed so exciting. What did she really think of me? What did she do when she wasn't in the library?

For a second when I get to the library, I hesitate. Will she think I'm strange coming back again so soon? I could take a walk to the old junkyard and look for interesting things, but I don't. I go inside. She is behind the counter just like yesterday. I ask her if she wants to take a walk with me, and she says sure, in an hour she can take lunch. While I'm waiting, I walk around the neighborhood, past where my childhood friend Lou-Lou lived. Lou-Lou abandoned me for no particular reason when we were ten. It was brutal and all in one swift thrust. One moment we were best friends, and the next week she wouldn't answer the phone when I called and sat with the powerful Laura Brody at lunch instead of with me. After a week of this, I took her a Slim Jim, like I had done so often, but I had to walk across the lunchroom to offer it, and with each step I felt more shame. When I offered it, extending the plastic shrink-wrapped meat stick, she told me that she didn't like Slim Jims, even though she had always loved them before. For the longest time I didn't know why she had rejected me, but one day a few months later, I saw her alone at the playground.

"Why won't you talk to me, Lou-Lou?" I asked.

"You're too strange," she said. "I want to be friends with Laura, and I can't be friends with you both."

And just like that, four years of friendship was gone. Later, Lou-Lou became a cheerleader and was on the prom court. Somehow at ten she sensed that our paths were going in different directions.

I take Rose for a walk by the river. We pass the church where my mother used to take me for Sunday school as a kid. I remember the struggle in my mind caused by the plaster rendering of Christ on the cross in the sanctuary. He was in such pain—blood coming from his hands and feet, an open wound on his chest—that it was hard to pay attention to anything that was said in that room. In Sunday school we made paper arks for the animals, and the teacher reenacted on a felt board the story of the loaves and fishes, and we sang songs about Jesus loving the little children, but when I went to the big church and saw the nails going straight through his palms, I knew what church was really about.

Rose and I walk next to the river, where it smells like sperm this time of year. I'm not sure why, but there is grass everywhere, and liquids oozing out of things, and the only thing I can compare the weird scent to is sperm. Then we pass a terrible smelling tree everyone calls a pukeberrry tree, and it blots out the smell of sperm with the smell of vomit. Still, I love it here. In this spot the river is fat and slow and a chocolate brown, with trees leaning over into it, almost swampy at the edges. I stare into the water, imagining myself a female Huck Finn, floating with the current to some adventure. And then I think of everything, as looking at water makes you do. How we are on this planet. How this is what is real—the river, the ground, the sky—and everything else is an illusion.

"This is really pretty," Rose says. "I haven't been down here yet."

"The river is the best place here," I say.

"Why do you like it so much?" she asks, smiling.

"I guess it's always given me a feeling of being tied to the rest of the world. We're not so cut off here. Plus it's just always been my place." How do I describe that here I feel alive and everywhere else I feel like the walking dead?

"Do you think it's special because you live here, or would you feel that way about it even if you lived somewhere else?" she asks.

She sits on some grass by the bank. There are some mallard ducks nearby. I like that she just sits down without looking and doesn't worry about her clothes.

"I don't know. I guess I like it because it's here and I'm here."

I sit next to her.

"That's not a bad thing," she says.

This close to the river, I don't smell the semen and puke, just a little funk, a bit like the smell of death, but with a breeze. The trees nearby are swaying. Everything is moving. The river is moving, the trees are moving, my heart is moving.

"What about other rivers?" Rose asks. "Do you think there is a river where you would just feel something special about it, even the first time you saw it? The Ganges is considered sacred, and people swim in it even though it's full of pollution and raw sewage and everything."

"Have you been there?"

I imagine all of the places that Rose may have been, and all of the places I haven't. I imagine, but I am here, in this place, and she is here too.

"No, but I want to go," she says.

"When I was a kid I used to imagine that if I wanted to get away on the river, I could, like Huck Finn—just steal a boat or make a raft and sail away, but girls don't do that. And if I disappeared, my mother would think I was kidnapped and sexually abused."

"It's true. You can't really run away when you're a kid anymore, especially not a girl. It's too dangerous."

Rose looks at me, and I can't tell what she's thinking.

"I tried to move my interest to survivalism," I say. "Sometimes I read books on how to find edible things to eat in the wild, like cattails and fiddlehead ferns."

"Did you ever eat them?"

"No, I was too afraid of getting poisoned. I still think a fiddlehead fern sounds pretty good, though. I like the way they kind of uncurl themselves, like waking babies."

Rose's smile widens. "I like it here," she says. "I like thinking about what makes a place special and whether it's in the place or in the way we see it."

"Did you ever read *The Little Prince*?" I ask.

I notice the dappled light on her face, creating a pattern on her cheeks. She picks up a few leaves and puts them on her knee. A red one and a yellow one.

"I saw the movie," she says.

"The movie was really creepy, but in the book there is a part where the little prince meets a fox, and the fox says the prince can't play with him because he isn't tame. He says that right now the prince means nothing to him, but if the prince comes back every day, then he will become special to the fox over time. He teaches the little prince how to tame him . . . and when the fox goes away, he says he will think of the little boy whenever he sees wheat, because of his golden hair."

"So you think the river is the same?"

"Maybe, somehow. Maybe to a stranger the river doesn't look like much, but if you come back every day, it starts to tame you. I don't know." Suddenly I feel embarrassed from all of this talking.

"Yes," Rose says, "I can see that. Being tamed sounds nice."

She picks up a small flat rock and throws it onto the water. It actually skips three times, like magic. How did she do that? I can never make a stone skip. I look at her arms. They are muscular, and her hands are long and graceful.

I see a man across the river who looks homeless. There was only one homeless man in our town when I was a kid. He wasn't really homeless, I guess. He lived in a tiny shack about five feet square near the river, but I think he's dead now. This man is walking with a dog. He doesn't see us. I feel a shiver up my spine as I remember warnings my mother gave me about going to the river by myself. I always had the fear that something here would get me, that I would be pushed into the water, or I would get my feet caught in something and drown, or accidentally dive into a huge rock, or be pulled by an invisible hand to the bottom. They would find me in the grass, a dead body. Something about being a young girl made it seem inevitable I'd end up dead by the river. The river, where all of the bodies end up.

I start asking Rose questions, and one question leads to another. I grill her about her family. I want to know everything about her, and over the next hour I find out the core of Rose's history. We are talking and everything is pouring out and time is going so quickly and I feel like I have never really talked to someone like this before. It's so easy and so deep so fast.

I learn that Rose has a mother and a stepfather and a stepmother, and her father lives in another state and has a new baby who Rose thinks is cute but doesn't really see very much. She doesn't particularly think of the baby as a sibling because it's so little and her stepmother is young and kind of trailer trash and Rose is a bit ashamed of the whole situation. Her father will never grow up. Her father is Italian, and her mother is Taiwanese. Rose has been on her own since she was sixteen and moved out because her mom was fucked up and trying to control her and definitely was not okay with who Rose was. She has worked since then and decided to become a librarian because it is stable and she loves books. So she paid her way through community college, college, and library school by working as a waitress, which she does not have the natural temperament for, but was able to succeed by getting hired at high-end restaurants where people want you to be a little rude to them. She left Philadelphia because all of her friends were crazy and into drugs and she wanted to just be someplace mellow. Then Rose adds that she also left Philly because of a bad breakup with her girlfriend.

When she says this, I feel lightness in my body, like a relief, like I knew this already and was waiting for it. I realize I have known all along somehow that Rose is a lesbian.

"I think I'm more mature than she is," she says about her ex. "She's like one of those girls who is never sure of herself."

I hope I'm not one of those girls. Am I? Suddenly I want to change my whole life so that Rose doesn't think I'm immature. "What do your parents think about you being a lesbian?" I ask.

Rose laughs. "We don't talk about it too much. My stepfather thinks it's a passing stage, but I also think he was a little in love with my last girlfriend. He sort of checked her out a lot and made her feel nervous. He told her she should be having babies. I think he would have liked to be the father. You know, a volunteer sperm donor. Yuck," she says.

"That must have made her uncomfortable."

"Not really. Nothing made Lizzy uncomfortable. She was formidable, but she looked femme. She came from a really fucked-up family, so she thought my stepfather was nice. It's like if your father is an abusive ass-hole who has sex with you when you're thirteen, then somebody who is just an insensitive jerk seems nice. But I actually get along better with him than I do with my mother. My mother doesn't really like me much. I was such a burden to her, stole her youth."

"She must like you," I say. "She's your mother."

"Not all mothers like their children, Claudia."

"I think they do, deep down, under it all."

"No, not really," she says. "My mother was eighteen when I was born, and she wanted to go to college but couldn't because of me, and she married someone she thought was an idiot, and they were very unhappy. She wanted to be an actress, and she was very pretty and thin before I came along and ruined her figure. She probably wouldn't have ever really been an actress, but she had fantasies."

"Did she tell you that?"

"Yes. Many times. She would show me pictures of how she looked before I was born and after. There were no photos of her pregnant with me; that was not considered a Kodak moment. She's vain. That's what my mother is. I think if it had been a different time, she would have gotten rid of me and probably been happier."

"She worked at a factory?'

"On the assembly line. Light factory work. But even if she hadn't had me, I don't think she could have been a model. That kind of dream is delusional. Anyway, that's my mother."

"Was she mean to you?" I ask.

"No, not really. She wasn't abusive. She always took care of me physically. My father always liked me and played with me, though he never took parenting very seriously. My mother was dead serious about everything. She made sure my clothes were clean and she fed me and she watched so that I didn't kill myself accidentally, but she never really liked me. She was just some angry person who never said anything. She was always thinking about her dream and wanting to move to New York. I wish she could forgive me. I guess I always tried to not make much trouble, hoping she would forget that I was around and maybe have some fun. I felt like I was the thing that spoiled her life."

Rose looks so beautiful and confident and incapable of spoiling anyone's life. I don't understand how anyone can be as stupid as Rose's mom.

Finally Rose turns to me and says, "I need to get back to work, and I'm tired from talking so much."

We get up and start back. I walk close to Rose, hoping to smell her, to see what her special scent is. I remember one day in grade school, when we were eight, Lou-Lou and I smelled each other deeply and promised to remember each other's special scent forever, and then even if aliens changed our faces and our actions, we could still identify each other's smell and be able to tell who we really were.

When Rose is close, I catch a little of her scent. She smells like books and ink and citrus and a funny smell that must be *her* smell, underneath it all, a little musky, a little peppery, a tiny bit funky.

Rose stops and looks at me. "What are you doing?"

I laugh nervously. "Smelling you," I say.

"Is there something wrong with how I smell?"

"No, I'm sorry. I just wanted to see what you smelled like."

"Are we at that stage of the relationship?" she asks and laughs a short, dry laugh. "Nobody has asked me so many questions so quickly in a long time," she says. "Will you remember any of it?"

"Yes," I say. "Everything. Quiz me."

She smiles. "You're so sweet. Does everyone here talk like this, so sincerely and really wanting to listen?"

"No, nobody but me," I say, and Rose laughs again.

"Well, I guess I'll have to hang out with you then," she says.

I nod, and for some reason, when we walk up from the bank of the river, I take Rose's hand. It's like we are school friends, walking together, linked by our hands. Some of her fingers feel rough. She has some band-aids here and there, maybe from paper cuts, and I am careful not to hurt her.

# THINKING OF ROSE

That night, lying in my bed, I rub a pillow between my legs and think about Rose. She is a prison guard, and I have entered the women's prison. I imagine her wearing a green uniform, her hair up in a bun. She is very stern, with the repressed look of sadistic prison guards everywhere. The prison seems to be quite empty except for us. She has to search me before I can enter the area where the cells are. She tells me she needs to check me very carefully in private. We go to her office, where there is a metal table, and she tells me to sit on the table while she searches me.

Is she even Rose in the fantasy? I usually only have fantasies about aliens or strangers, or if there is a particular person, it's a generic version of them. The guard looks like Rose but is acting in a way I don't think Rose would act. Even so, it will be hard to look at Rose later without thinking of her in this role. It will be hard to face her.

Rose has a club in her hand and is running it over my body, checking for contraband. I feel the hardness of the club against my breasts, along my stomach, between my legs. I open my thighs wider so she knows I am not smuggling anything, and she runs the club along my panties, against the lips of my pussy. I am wearing a plain gray dress, and she gets down on her knees under my skirt and is feeling with her hands for anything between my legs. She starts unbuttoning my dress and runs her fingers under my clothes and inside of my underwear. As she inspects me for weapons, she cups her breasts with my hands.

# CHINESE POISONING

Recently I read in the newspaper about a mass food poisoning in China. I saved the story in my poison notebook. Sometimes I save stories I am too afraid to read, like articles about mad cow disease. It's like worrying a sore spot in your mouth. I am afraid if I start to read about mad cow disease, I may make myself insane, but I won't know if I'm insane because of fear that I have mad cow disease or if I really have it and the disease is causing me to go insane. But this story wasn't about mad cow; it was a story of conventional poisoning, which I have less fear of, so I could read it. (I define conventional poisoning as the kind where a person knows they've been poisoned shortly after it happens, rather than the kind of poisoning that works secretly over time. Secretly over time I can't deal with. There is a mushroom that you can eat, for example, that won't kill you for two weeks—my mind can't even go there.)

When I first heard of the incident in China on the radio, the story was still progressing. This was very satisfying; I followed the news like a baseball game. At first they didn't know for sure how many people were dead. Maybe forty, maybe eighty. (There was an election coming up in China, and nobody wanted to talk about it. Papers said *dozens* to be inexactly accurate.) Later I found out that the victims were mostly students going to a breakfast snack shop. Fried dough sticks, sesame cakes, and glutinous rice seemed to be the culprits. The illness started so soon that people were literally dropping in the streets after leaving the shop. It was some kind of poison, but they didn't know if it was intentional. I believed it was accidental. I trusted the breakfast shop owner. I kept checking the radio throughout the day. Most food poisoning takes time to work in the body, so it was odd how quickly people were getting sick.

The Chinese government warned journalists to stay away, but gradually the details came out. The first reports were that it might be bad oil or some natural pathogen. Those were followed by suspicions of rat poison. Finally it was revealed that the man responsible for the poisonings was a cousin of the pastry shop owner. He owned a rival snack shop and was jealous of the success of Zengwu Pastry Bar. He used a type of poison no longer manufactured, which would translate as Super Strong Rat Poison. It turned out it was a revenge poisoning, which (according to the journalists, at least) is not uncommon in China.

# SWADDLE

Rose and I have started spending all our free time together. She's like my best friend, but something more. It's as though electricity builds up between us. We start hanging out and don't stop. I go to her house and we watch old movies or we take walks in the woods. I love her pink house and how cozy everything is.

I am sitting in her living room, which is filled with rugs and blankets and pillows like a nest, and she is reading. Her face is bent over a book, and I think of all of the great paintings of women reading, and how the look of someone you desire concentrating on something else is so exciting, when she is only half here, her mind in Moscow with *The Master and Margarita*.

"Have you ever fallen in love with someone in a book?" I ask her.

"Sure. I was in love with the married woman in *Written on the Body*. I wanted someone to be obsessed with me like that."

"Were you jealous?" I ask.

"A little. It felt like they were the only two people in the world, and when the other woman left, her absence colored everything. When I was younger I really wanted that kind of intensity. I wanted to be the only thing in the world for someone else." She smiles thinking about it and shakes her head. "Have you been in love with a character?" she asks.

"Never really a character, but an author. I hate to admit it, but I was in love with Stephen Crane. I read him when I was in seventh grade, and I thought he was the most sensitive writer, someone who really cared about the world. Have you ever read *Maggie: A Girl of the Streets*?"

"No, I read *Red Badge*."

"Yeah, that's his most famous book. I liked that one too because he was so thoughtful about the war and suffering, but *Maggie* is about a girl growing up in New York. She's from a really poor family, and she starts sleeping with her brother's friend and then becomes a prostitute."

"I guess that sounds kind of sexy," Rose says. "Not really my thing, though."

"I liked the harshness and realism of it, but I also felt like the author really cared about Maggie. He had a lot of empathy. Maybe it's a little warped. I don't know. He also wrote poetry. In high school I thought it was great, but now it seems silly."

"Do you remember it?"

"Yeah." I blush.

"Tell me," she says.

She is standing in front of me now and looking into my eyes. I have managed to get her to put down her book, which makes me sad and happy. I like to see her reading, but then I want her to look at me. It must be this drive that makes people want to be writers.

I start my recitation, feeling like a thirteen-year-old. "A man said to the universe: 'Sir, I exist!' 'However,' the universe replied, 'The fact has not created in me a sense of obligation.'" I pause for a second. "That's it."

"I can see loving that as a teenager." She smiles.

"Yeah, it has a certain philosophical coldness. There's another, too."

"Do you want to lie down?" she asks.

I think this means we are really going to talk now, so we should get comfortable. I follow her to the bedroom, where we settle down on her bed together. She is resting her hand under her head, half sitting up. I am lying on my back, my head on a pillow but turned to face her.

There is bright light shining in the window, and I notice the gold highlights in her eyes. I lie close to her, but not touching. Lately I've noticed a kind of forcefield around our bodies. When we get too close, I can't think. I can feel her next to me, even though there's no physical contact.

"It's nice lying here," she says, holding my gaze.

I'm suddenly nervous. There is a fly buzzing around the room, and I think of Emily Dickinson's poem about dying and hearing a fly buzz and how everything important and mundane is mixed up. Rose's lips look dry.

I feel my hands at my sides and my legs inside of my jeans, and I feel my breasts underneath my shirt and my bra, and I feel my ears, a little tingly, and an itch in the backs of my eyes, as if they are pushing out of my head a little, and my breath as it comes into my body and gets stuck a little in my throat. I feel the warmth of Rose next to me, but I can't touch her.

Rose turns on her side, facing me. "Tell me the other poem," she says.

"It's really melodramatic," I say, "but here goes: 'Many red devils ran from my heart and out upon the page, they were so tiny the pen could mash them. And many struggled in the ink. It was strange to write in this red muck of things from my heart.'"

I finish and realize I'm blushing. She is still looking at me intently. I'm afraid she might kiss me, and then I don't know what might happen.

"Wow, that's where it's at," she says. "How beautifully melodramatic."

Rose moves her hair in back of her neck, a gesture she often makes. She takes a pillow and puts it on my stomach and rests her elbow on top of it. I think of the swaddling fantasy. I think about asking her to do it, but I'm embarrassed. I get quiet.

"What are you thinking about?" she says.

"I don't know," I say. My mouth opens, but I have a hard time saying it.

"What?" she says. "Look, you opened your mouth. What were you going to say?"

"Will you do something for me?"

"Sure, what?" she says.

"There is this thing I've always wanted to do. I'm a little nervous and afraid it's too much to ask."

"What is it?"

She is inches from me, and I notice that she has a mole with a hair in it at the base of her neck. Her lips also have some dry patches on them. I like seeing her slight imperfections.

"You know when you're a baby and your mother puts blankets really tight against you so you can't move. It's called swaddling."

"You want me to do that?"

She looks a little puzzled. Have I freaked her out? Does she think I'm too weird?

I nod.

"Well, why not?" she says.

She gathers the pillows from the bed, then goes into the living room and gets some from the couch. I'm still lying on the bed, on top of the comforter, and she lifts the edges of the comforter and wraps it around my body, then puts the pillows against my sides. I tell her to put the pillows so tight against me that I can't move, and she does. She is gathering more pillows from all over the house, placing them on either side of my head and all up and down my body, and then she gets on the bed. She takes off her shoes. She is wearing jeans and a soft t-shirt, not her library clothes. She has her hair back in a ponytail, and it makes her look very young, almost childlike. I love the rigorous, exact way she is lining up the pillows. She feels like a mother and a nurse. She feels like a lover. She bundles me up and I am tight inside and then she puts her arms around the pillows and squeezes. Her body is almost on top of me while she's doing this, and her face is so close. She is half lying and half sitting and squeezing me.

"Tight enough?" she asks.

"Tighter," I say.

She squeezes me more, and her face so close to mine makes me nervous, and I feel not just comforted but aroused.

I want to kiss her lips.

I close my eyes, and this is what it feels like to be a little baby; this is what it feels like to have no way out and not be afraid. This is how it feels to be wrapped up by another and taken care of. God, this feels good. I can't move. I can't do anything. Nothing is expected of me. This is exactly the feeling I wanted.

After she has swaddled me for a while, I start to feel guilty. "Hey, Rose," I say. "Thank you. You can stop now. I don't want you to get tired."

"It's fun," she says. "Are you my little baby?"

"Yes," I say. "Thank you. You are the best swaddler ever."

"You're welcome," she says and kisses me on the forehead. It feels like a burn mark where her lips have been.

*game seven*

# RARE BOOKS

Imagine that you are a book, the kind of book that is very rare. You are a leather-bound book with gold embossed letters on your cover and spine, but it's what's inside you that is most important. I have been searching for you for a long time, maybe forever. I look in the rare-book sections of libraries, but I can't find you. I look in bookstores everywhere. When I am traveling in Turkey or London, I stop at booksellers randomly and hope that you will be on the shelf, but you never are. You elude me. You are hiding somewhere in a basement or on a shelf among innumerable stacks of paper. I have read in another book, whose name I no longer remember, that you exist. I am not sure what I am going to find in you, but I know it is something I need. Do you understand? The one thing that I need is inside your pages, and I can't find you.

And then maybe, when I'm seventy-three and have forgotten all about you, and I'm in a little town, off the map, the kind of place that nobody cares about, where the only official history of the town is a long-forgotten, eighty-year-old volume, I find you. You are right there, under my nose, perhaps left on a bus or on the floor of a thrift shop—or a stranger hands you to me and says, "Here. I didn't like this, but you might."

*I didn't like this.* Meaning *this was not magical for me. For me, this was not what they write the operas about, but for you, for you, it might be.*

I hold you in my hands, I read your words. Your words are in my mouth. I eat your words. Your words are inside of me. I stroke your leather binding, your gold embossing, your pages, your paper like a drug, so smooth under my fingers, thick and heavy, more like cloth than paper, something I could use as a bandage in an emergency. And when I read you, will you make a difference? Is there something in you that will excite me?

# DINNER AT MY HOUSE

I am lying on the floor of my bathroom. It's cool with my head against the tiles. I notice a tampon that has rolled behind the toilet and think about how they always roll everywhere. Rose is in the other room, sitting on the couch, waiting for me. I feel nauseous, my stomach fluttery, my bowels contorting and my heart beating a little faster than normal. Am I poisoned? Have I poisoned Rose? She is in the living room, wearing a green dress that looks very nice on her, her bare arms showing, the muscles in them clear and her skin soft and shiny, slightly sweaty, drinking a glass of red wine that doesn't taste that good, which I picked because there was a woman in a blue dress on the bottle. She is perfectly lovely (both the woman on the bottle and Rose), but I'm here on the bathroom floor. I have diarrhea, and I don't know if it was the food I ate—the food that I cooked, the food that I served Rose. If I have poisoned her, then we might both die.

I spent all day cooking, making Indian food from recipes in a book. I couldn't find papadum and some of the spices in BigTown, but I managed to get the majority of the ingredients: garam masala and curry . . . and turmeric, which left an awful yellow stain on my bathrobe, but even then I was deliriously happy when I started cooking for Rose.

I had to drive to a little ethnic food store in the city for some things. It seemed like the stuff there had been on the shelves a long time, and the man behind the counter was talking on the phone, so I couldn't really ask him any questions. He just looked over my things and added it up in his head and told me the price, not stopping his conversation, saying to the person on the phone, "I just don't trust him. I don't trust him." I don't know who he didn't trust, but his untrusting left me not trusting him. Still, I had the ingredients for the recipes.

On the bathroom floor, I admit to myself that the fact that I spent all day making the meal means I want to have sex with Rose. Why else would I cook all day? There are things that you do for friends—like make spaghetti or cheese toast with tomato—and then there are things you do for lovers. Ever since Rose swaddled me, I've felt like we've moved to this other level, where I have shown her something about myself and there is no going back. I like looking at her for no reason, and when we go to the movies I have a feeling of awkwardness, of wanting her to reach out and touch me, of being super aware of her body in the dark next to me. So this is lust; I know that. But what should I do with it, and why do I feel so nervous? What if I make a move and the move goes nowhere? What if I am just fantasizing about what being with Rose is like and then I don't really want all of it? To make things worse, I have been avoiding Hal as if I were unfaithful to him, as if I even could be unfaithful to someone fifty-seven years older than me whom I kissed once.

I tried to make dinner perfect. I even made paneer, which I have eaten once at an Indian restaurant but had no idea one could make oneself until I read page 167 of *Indian Cooking for Everyone*. Indian cooking may be for everyone, but by the time you make paneer, naan, curry, and rice, you are so exhausted you don't even want to eat the food. Every one of my pots and pans is dirty, and I had to borrow a pan from Fran because I ran out. I told Fran I was making dinner for a friend, and she said that cooking for others is a great pleasure. She's so sweet sometimes.

Another thing I think about on the bathroom floor is how cooking can lead to poisoning. I put some coconut milk in the curry, but I had my doubts about the coconut milk. The label on the can was green and had a coconut on it, but it didn't say anything in English, and it smelled funny. I tried to find an expiration date, but there was only an odd string of numbers on the bottom that didn't seem to mean anything. I thought, *Don't be silly. It's okay.* I was listening to the radio, which was playing "I Heard It Through the Grapevine," and I was feeling light and carefree, mixing things and making my kitchen absolutely messy, with flour on the floor from the naan, which turned out really good, and several pots bubbling on the stove, and the paneer being drained through cheese-cloth, which I had never used before and reminded me of bandages. With the cheese mixture draining through the white fabric, I felt like I had some kind of small injured body that I was taking care of. It was all going well until I looked at the clock and realized that Rose would arrive in ten minutes. Then I felt a flutter in my stomach.

I was gripped with a desire to throw away everything I'd made. But then what would we have for dinner, and how would I explain the mess to Rose? I could pull out a frozen pizza, but nobody would believe all of this mess was created for that. I spooned up some cauliflower curry, and it tasted good; the worst poisons always taste the best.

Through dinner, I played it cool and tried to believe I was not poisoning Rose, but now here I am. I don't know if I am sick because of the coconut milk or because I might have sex with Rose tonight. I've been having fears that we are headed in that direction, and I don't know what that direction means. My stomach feels rubbed raw, and I try to soothe it by making little circles on it with my flat hand.

I can't stay in the bathroom much longer. I notice the dirt in the cracks of the tiles, a pile of hairs on the edge of the bathtub, and on the floor a stray toilet paper roll, hair tie, and two lipstick tubes. My apartment is filthy. I myself feel dirty, with cheese juice dripped on my skirt and turmeric under my fingernails and some bread dough in my hair. How can I be so messy?

What are the possible effects of bad coconut milk? Can botulism grow in this environment?

I start to get up, and then lie down again, my stomach cramping. The cool of the floor is soothing. I know I must get up or Rose will start to worry about me. What if she knocks on the door, and I'm on the floor in here? I couldn't explain it.

I pick up one of the lipstick tubes and read the color like an augury: Frosted Pearl. That sounds boring. I pick up the other one. This is my true omen, I think. Scarlet Velvet—I like that. Sort of like an old movie star, seductive. There is a very beautiful woman in my living room who would probably have sex with me if I pull myself together. What am I doing in here? I put on some Scarlet Velvet and get up.

Rose is still sitting on the couch, which is my mother's old couch before she bought the white one, reading a book of mine on astral projection. She's been looking at my books and has selected the most embarrassing one imaginable. I should have hidden that book the way I hid a few others that seemed especially incriminating, like *Common Poisons in Everyday Items* and *Overcoming Obsessive Thoughts*.

She doesn't seem to notice I've been in the bathroom a long time. She is smiling at me like this is still a normal date, because of course she doesn't know what's going on in my mind.

"Have you tried to astral project?" she asks.

"Not really," I say. "Well, a little, but I never got out of my body."

"Why do you want to get out of your body?"

She has put down the book. Does she know that she has a way of looking at me that makes me nervous?

"I don't know. See what it's like out there. Travel to other places."

"Do you think there is a *you* without the body?"

"I guess I do," I say. "Do you?"

"I don't know," she says. "I think that I am this body, but there might be something else that isn't me inside my body. Do you think astral projection is your way of trying to escape this town without leaving?"

"I never thought about it, but maybe. I would really just like to escape to another world."

I sit next to her, only a few inches away. She doesn't seem to be poisoned. She isn't sick. My stomach is settling a little. Her leg is touching mine, and it's like a small shock.

"If you could go anywhere, where would you go?" I ask.

"I think I'd like to go to India. It's so much more spiritually advanced."

"That would be nice," I say.

We are talking, but really everything that is going on is this movement of energy between us, her body drawing me closer, my fear keeping me apart. Who will win the battle?

"We have some of the same books," she says, and my stomach eases a bit more.

"You've been looking at all of my books while I was in the bathroom," I say with a slight tone of accusation.

"Of course. I'm a librarian. I could help you some with categorization, you know."

"Oh, there are no categories. Just wherever I can fit something on the shelf or stack on the floor."

"You have a lot of good books. I love Russian novels too, and all of the Jung and anthropology. Great stuff. I also noticed a lot of books about poisoning." Her voice is a question.

"Yes." I nod. "That's an interest of mine."

I'm trying not to give away too much too soon. If I start talking about poison, it will kill the romance for sure.

"You're a little eccentric, aren't you?" she says.

"Maybe," I say.

"I like that about you," she says.

She is leaning over toward me. She puts her hand on my shoulder and starts playing with the ends of my hair. Her touch sends small electric currents to the rest of my body.

"Can I kiss you?" she says.

*My God, yes*, I think. *Of course. I want you to.* "Sure," I say softly.

She smells like mint and walnuts and curry. Her mouth feels like a cat's, kind of raspy and small. She is giving me small kisses all over my lips.

I lean into her and kiss her more deeply. Time speeds up and slows down and I don't know if I will make it through the night alive.

Rose pulls back and gazes at me intensely, and I feel like she is looking inside my head.

I'm afraid she sees all the confusion in there—that I want to be with her but don't know how, and the fear that she is so close, so very close to me.

Then I am kissing her again, and it feels good and her lips are so soft, pushing into my lips, her tongue pushing into me, and she is running her hands over my clothes, feeling my body through them and I have my hand on the side of her face and can feel her hair falling over my fingers like silk threads, and I am running my hand over her skin and her hair and she is leaning into me, and now I can feel her breasts under her clothes, feel the softness of her pushing against me. Her mouth is on my neck now, and I want to swoon back, it feels so delicious how she is making little kisses on my throat, and I am leaning back and my mouth is open and I am pulling her on top of me.

*game eight*

# MAGICAL SOUP

Rose and I live in a cave together deep in the mountains. She is always cooking something magical—something to make us wise or to make us powerful. She gives me something to eat. It's from a vat of gray stuff that she has been mixing all day.

"Is that safe?" I ask her.

"Don't you trust me, baby?" she says.

When she says *trust* it sends a small shiver up my spine. The word *trust* next to the word *baby* makes me ill.

"I don't know," I say. "Should I?"

Does anyone ever really trust their lover completely? Maybe she is trying to poison me. Maybe she wants me dead so that she can do something with my body. Trust comes hard to me.

"Does it have bat in it?" I ask.

"No, it doesn't."

She looks so beautiful and youthful sitting there. And honest, I guess.

"Is it just a little bit poisonous, like blowfish?" I ask.

"No," she says. "I love you. You can trust me. See? I'm taking a bite."

She eats a spoonful of the gray stuff. Then she feeds some to me. It is the color of gutters and industrial rivers and rainbow-streaked oil puddles, but I taste it anyway since she is feeding it to me.

It tastes wonderful—nutty and deep and rich and smoky. I should have trusted her all along. She feeds it to me in spoonfuls and then in bowlfuls, and I can't get enough of it.

"What is it?" I ask.

"It's truffle soup."

"Does it have magical powers?"

"No, it just tastes good," she says.

It's the best soup I have ever had. I eat until it's all gone, and then I want more, but there is no more. Rose holds me in her arms, and I drowse like someone very satisfied with their meal. But I am getting so sleepy and dreamy so quickly that I think it may have been poisoned after all. Don't the most poisonous things sometimes taste the best? I look at her holding me. Did she poison me? Will I ever wake up?

# A PARTY OF LIBRARIANS

Rose has invited me to a party, a party of librarians, or more precisely a party with a few librarians, some library assistants, friends of the library, and other volunteers. They are having a party for her since she is new to the job. I want to go, but I have to face the fact that I've been mean to Hal since I started sleeping with Rose. I have purposely avoided seeing him, never going to the library when I know he'll be there. It's awkward because I kissed him, and then I met Rose, and I didn't expect that to happen. This isn't the kind of thing that has ever happened to me—a relationship. I think I can say that Rose and I have a relationship, whatever that means. Now my flirtation with Hal is something I just want to forget, but he will be at the party. I'm nervous to face him with Rose.

Rose picks me up in her old green Nova. The party is a little bit out in the country, in an old farmhouse that Cindy McGuff has fixed up for her family, complete with all of the faux country charms. Cindy is a volunteer at the library.

Rose is wearing a purple shirt that makes her look beautiful. Lately I've become obsessed with how beautiful Rose is. Something about the shirt brings out the color of her hair and skin. Her hair is slicked down, and she looks like she is going to an event much more exciting than this one. I want to touch her.

"Hey, you look like a big city girl," I say. "You're going to blow these hicks out of the water."

"Thanks."

She smiles, and there is something mysterious in the curve of her mouth. Sometimes Rose seems so clear to me, and sometimes she seems like a totally unknown creature. I'm not sure what role I am playing at this party.

"So am I your girlfriend or your friend?" I ask.

"Does it matter?" she says teasingly.

"Well, it might matter if I put my hand on your waist or kiss you or something. It might matter to the librarians."

She drives out of Riverton and down a country road. We pass an old dairy that still has a few cows lazing around. It dipped below freezing last night, and there is a layer of frost on the ground. A lot of the countryside around us is gradually becoming housing developments, but here and there old farms are still hanging on.

"Librarians are very open-minded."

"Not around here."

The road winds down near the river, and I see some ice forming on the trees. Soon it will be snowing, and I'll feel like I want to hide out inside, build a fort in my bed against the elements.

"Let's leave it ambiguous, but no touching," she says.

"But you look good. I want to touch you."

"Yeah, everybody does."

Rose has a way of appearing perfectly confident that is amazing to me. I watch her drive, leaning back in my seat, and she puts on a Tracy Chapman song, "Fast Car," and I think we could drive like this forever.

But we get there in fifteen minutes. For some reason I have not told Rose about Hal. I'm not hiding it; it's just that it's complicated and weird to explain. I don't want her to think I'm confused. Since I've met Rose, what I had with Hal seems immature. I guess even though I'm honest with Rose, I'm interested in her seeing me in a good light, not as some kind of crazy kid who gets crushes on grandfatherly librarians.

Hal is standing next to the crackers and onion dip when I get there. He is the first person I see after Cindy, who is pregnant and wearing a pink hostess dress, the kind of thing Jackie O wore when was pregnant. Hal looks surprised to see me, and then he takes in that I'm with Rose and seems confused.

Rose walks over to him and introduces us, and I bite the inside of my mouth.

"Oh, Rose, we know each other," I say.

"Right. How could I forget? You're a library regular. You probably know more people here than I do."

Hal smiles. "Glad to see that you two girls have become friends."

When he says *girls*, I feel a slight prickliness at my neck. Will Rose think he's sexist? My stomach makes movements like a wave machine. I'm trying to figure out if there is a double meaning in what he said or if he is just being friendly and naïve. Rose smiles back. She seems genuinely happy, and I feel amazed that I could actually make her happy.

People are talking about their gardens and a new restaurant in town and other boring topics. I thought they would be talking about books more, but they're not.

In the corner of the room I see June Groff, the woman who always lectured me about overdue books. Her hair is that shade of blue that older woman sometimes have, and she is wearing a blue church dress. She is eating from a plate piled high with crackers and cheese, spinach dip, and artichoke dip. She is moving the calories and fat to her mouth quickly. She sees me and waves and actually smiles. I walk toward her, anticipating a lecture about something I am doing wrong. I can hear her saying, "Aren't you the Hecht girl? Are you a lesbian? What would your mother think about your being a lesbian?"

"Hello, Miss Groff," I say. "How are you?" She actually seems happy to see me. She is old now and seems happy to just be alive and eating.

"Claudia, isn't it?" she says. I nod. "You really love the library, don't you? I remember you coming from the time you were a kid."

"Yes," I say, "I do."

"Why aren't you a librarian?" she says.

I just smile at her and say, "I never thought of it."

"It's great to get to spend all of your life around books," she says.

I always thought she hated her job, but maybe she really loved it. Maybe when she was so mean about late books, she was just fiercely protecting the books like a mother bear protecting a cub. Or maybe she has mellowed with age. My nemesis is old and wearing dentures and won't be lecturing me anymore.

Hal is drinking a lot. I've never seen him drink before, and it's strange. He's talking to some of the women, going on about Heraclitus. I don't know how that came up. He seems to have a smattering of knowledge about almost everything. I overhear Cindy conversing with Rose. Cindy looks a bit tired, like the hostess duties are too much on top of her pregnancy, but she is smiling hard.

"What do you think of Riverton?" She spreads cheese on crackers and picks up some stray paper plates as she talks.

"Oh, it's nice. I like it," Rose responds.

"It must seem awfully boring compared to Philly." Cindy stacks the plates on top of each other in a neat pile.

"Well, it's quiet, yeah." Rose is drinking a glass of red wine, quickly.

Cindy pours more chips into a bowl. "I guess you'll be moving along when you find a better job."

"I'm not sure. I like it here."

"Maybe you'll meet a nice guy. Settle down." Cindy stops pouring the chips and looks at Rose.

"Probably not," Rose says, very evenly and coolly. I admire her simple honesty. She's not shouting that she's a lesbian, but she's not playing any games either.

"You're not looking?" Cindy asks, her voice going up a little in disbelief.

"No," Rose says. She throws a quick glance at me that nobody would notice, or would they?

Cindy is silent. She is thinking.

I move through the party on my way to the deck outside. I put my hand on Rose's back as I pass her. Rose said not to touch, but I can't help it. I need them to know. Why? I feel a sense of exhilaration being here with her. I think, *I will have sex with this woman tonight.* It's like a secret I am holding inside my body.

On the deck I find Hal by himself. It's dark out here in the country, and you can see a lot of stars tonight with the moon a thin sliver. Hal is standing next to the railing and drinking something gold colored. Scotch, probably. I think about going back in but realize this is my chance to come clean with him.

"I haven't heard from you," he says when I approach. "Is everything all right?"

"Yes," I say. "I'm sorry I haven't called."

"You sure you're okay?" he asks.

"Yeah. I'm good. I'm really good," I say as my stomach sinks. I feel sick about being dishonest.

"Good," he says. "I was kind of worried after the death conversation—worried I was being too much of an amateur psychologist."

"No," I say. "It wasn't that. I liked that conversation. It's just I feel kind of strange. I guess I need to tell you something. I went to the library to see you after that conversation, and I met Rose, and we started talking." I pause. "I've kind of been seeing Rose."

"That's nice," he says. "She needs friends."

"More than friends," I say. I manage to look at him while I say this, to actually look at his face.

He seems uncomfortable. He nods a little. "You mean dating?"

"Yes."

"She's a lesbian?" He sits on a wooden rocking chair.

"Yeah," I say. I sit in the chair next to his. Now we are looking at the stars and the night, not face to face. The land behind the house consists of a meadow and some woods. I think I see something moving in the woods. A deer, maybe. I think how much easier it is to talk when you're not facing someone, like on a long car trip when you can tell someone your whole life without any eye contact.

"And you?" he asks.

"Not sure."

"Hmm," he says. He leans back in the rocker, and it makes a creaking noise.

"I'm sorry," I say. "I should have told you."

As Hal turns to me, he seems sad, but he still looks at me with warmth. "Claudia," he says, "I'm your friend. I'm too old to have my heart broken too badly. You had my mind whirling some, and I admit I am a bit smitten with you, but Rose is definitely more age-appropriate."

"I'm sorry if I led you on, Hal."

"Leading on is something teenage boys accuse teenage girls of doing. I am more than mature, unfortunately, and perfectly aware of the changeability of the human heart." His voice sounds dignified and kind.

"I'm so glad you're not angry at me," I say.

"I'm disappointed, but it was too good to be real." He winks at me. "Old men do get lonely, though. Don't avoid me now. "

"I won't," I say.

Rose comes outside with a young man I don't know. He's standing very close and moving his hands as he talks so that they are almost touching her. What's he doing? He is coming on to her. I feel a surge that starts in my eyes and runs down into my chest. He is looking at her like he wants to eat her, which makes me want to stab him with a knife. This is a terrible feeling. Is she responding to him? She's laughing in a nice way. I somehow thought she only laughed at my jokes. It's ridiculous, of course, to imagine she suppresses laughter at all other times. I feel a slight dizziness and a wave of anger. My God, I didn't know I was so jealous.

I walk over to Rose. I put my hand on her shoulder.

"Hi, Claude," she says.

"Hi, baby," I say and kiss her cheek.

Rose's eyes widen with surprise, and I think *I shouldn't be doing this.* The man watches us with intense interest.

# FATHER

Before he disappeared, the air kept getting thicker and thicker. That was the winter I never wanted to leave the house, thinking someone was going to attack me or corner me. A stray hair was a terrible sign (anything might be an omen), a car might zoom in front of me, or a paper cut might get arsenic in it and kill me.

There was already a feeling of doom surrounding me, so when the real doom finally came it seemed a patch of familiar darkness; I was attracted to the dark. I kept the lights out, hid in the closet, went to bed at eight o'clock, and in the morning lay in bed for hours, or until my mother banged on the door and said I would be late for school and she would not write me a note because I was not sick and she didn't write notes for pretenders. Half the time I didn't know if I was asleep or awake. I lingered so long in the in-between time, pretending to be asleep or trying to sleep or trying to stay awake so I could turn over and over the fears in my head. I was sure to have childhood cancer from the river, which I knew was like Love Canal, and my mother would probably die soon, and outside my window the pine trees lurked with spirits of the dead, and men wanted to kill young girls and hack up their bodies, and a man at the mall stared at me and asked if he could take my picture, and there would be a nuclear winter, and we should not be sleeping under blankets that could catch fire, but fireproof blankets had asbestos and would kill us. If there was a fire, I would stop, drop, and roll—but only if I was awake, and the *smoke* could kill me before I woke up, and we all know that people die from the smoke and not the fire. And my father's liver must look like a black sack filled with cirrhosis. He was, as everyone whispered, an alcoholic, and I had confirmed it for myself by reading the warning signs in *Reader's Digest* and checking off the answers on the quiz, and we as a family were firmly in denial. That made us all sick.

My father was rarely home that winter. When he did come home, it was early in the morning with the smell of alcohol and smoke on him. My mother waited up for him all night, every night, but when she heard his car, she slipped into bed and turned off the light.

In the middle of one night, I woke to the sound of pans banging in the kitchen. I came out of my room to see my mother—wearing a short blond wig, which she pulled on when she didn't feel like doing her hair—rolling the crust for an apple pie. She was using Bisquick, and later I realized she substituted Mrs. Butterworth's syrup for the brown sugar, because the apples tasted sickeningly mapley and sweet. We ate the pie in the morning for breakfast in huge slices, and my father was still not home when it was gone.

Meanwhile, my mother said nothing to my father. She did not yell. She did not ask questions. She was of the school of women who think they should not have to ask, and if she did ask for the simple things she deserved from her husband, like accounts of where he had been all night, then she would be lowered in some sense, brought down in her station as a good woman and wife.

The last time I saw my father, we had a terrible fight. At school that day, Mike Singer came up to me in the middle of the lunchroom, where I was sitting alone, eating meatloaf and some vegetable medley. He put a note on my tray next to my chocolate milk. The noise in the middle-school cafeteria was deafening, everyone talking around me, and I remember seeing him walking toward me, and then it was like in movies where everything fades out, because I knew what was coming. I mean, not literally, but I knew that *something* was coming, that his walking up to me was a bad omen, and then he put the note on my tray, which still contained the peas from the vegetable medley (peas are the only food that gives me the automatic vomit reflex). For some reason he had folded the note into a little shape, the way you fold love notes that you pass in class.

I'd never had a conversation with Mike Singer, but I knew who he was. He was the kind of guy who generally melted into his surroundings but that people thought of as nice. The one notable detail I remember about him was that he was a good cross-country runner. He threw the note on my tray and turned away, but before he left he gave me a look that had fear and doubt in it, a look of not wanting to do something but needing to.

I unfolded the note, which was written on lined school paper. His tiny chicken scrawl read: *Your father is having sex with my mother. I just thought you should know. Sincerely, Mike Singer.* I looked up, but he had disappeared back into the circus of the lunchroom, as if swallowed by a city crowd.

The words felt like a jab to my gut. I stared down at the chocolate milk in front of me and up at the rows and rows of kids eating their food and talking and pushing stuff around on their plates, and it all seemed very strange. It often felt like prison here, but now it was like I was in this other world.

There it was. I never doubted the truth of it. Why should I? His look was so real, so pained, that I knew it wasn't some joke. I knew Mike must feel as bad about the situation as I suddenly did. In fact, I have always liked Mike for writing me that note. In the terrible months that followed I even had fantasies of falling in love with Mike Singer, as if he could replace my father, but then I'd feel sick and wrong for imagining that, because the fact that my father and his mother had had sex would make it almost incest. I thought of finding him and just holding his hand, nothing more, but I never did—though after that day, whenever I saw him, a look passed between us, a look that said we knew something and that we were not going to talk about it, because to talk about it would be to open the door of our emotions, and that was a territory we didn't want to enter. I felt sick when I looked at him, even though we shared, or at least I think we shared, a bond of humiliation that put us in a special club together. At school sporting events or the mall when I would spot him and his sister or later him and his girlfriend, I would glance away and pretend I didn't see.

The day I got Mike's note, I went to talk to my father at his work bench, where he went to nail things together when he was home—always working on some project that he never finished—or where he cut up game from hunting. Once he had opened a slit in the stomach of a rabbit, showing me the corn it had eaten earlier that day. Now he looked surprised to see me. It was evening, and he was drinking beer, and there were four empty Buds in a row next to the bench. Dad had a big wad of chewing tobacco in his cheek. Next to him was a cup of liquid so black it could have been coffee, but it was his spit cup.

I put the note in front of him.

"Need me to sign something again?" he asked. Then he looked at it. His face got redder and he became agitated. He stared at it and then stared at me. He spit into the cup. "What is this shit?" he said. "You believe this shit?"

I was afraid to speak. I nodded. I noticed a small line of black saliva coming out the edge of his mouth.

"Jesus Christ." He ran his hands through his thinning hair. "You're a kid. What do you care about this? What's the matter with that Singer boy? What kind of sick mind does he have?"

He put away the piece of wood he was trying to make into a table. He must have felt the saliva, because he wiped his chin with the back of his hand. He looked old then, and I remember thinking that his skin was greasy, and he smelled like sweat and tobacco, and I couldn't understand why Mike's mother would want to have sex with him anyway. I hoped that he would deny it, say that it was all a lie, but I realized if he did I wouldn't believe him, so then I hoped he would confess to me, stop being a sinner or a liar and a drunk, and that maybe things could still be okay.

"Claudia," he said, "this is between your mother and me. You don't need to get involved in this. Just leave it be."

At his mention of my mother, I thought about how he sometimes laughed at her and said she was stupid. I felt dizzy with anger, like I'd been knocked in the head in a boxing match. I wanted to do something or say something that would hurt him, but I didn't know what. All I knew was that I'd clutched that note for hours, and it had taken all my reserves to confront him, and now I was as tired as I'd ever been. All of the weeks of waiting for doom fell like a black cloak over me, and I couldn't see anything but badness. I just looked at him and thought, *Why are you my father? I am nothing like you. You are a weak man, and you lie. I hate you.* That's the night I think I poisoned him.

# THE DOSE

We all knew about the river. We knew it was a mess of poison and strangeness and that the nuclear power plant there was bad. We knew, but we didn't say anything—because we also thought the river would save us. We thought it had the power to bring us something larger than this town: God, a story, a way out.

Everybody knew but pretended they didn't—about the river and the chemicals they were putting in it at the nuclear power plant. We knew that chemicals would seep into the river and into our drinking water and into us and we would be poisoned. Or I knew. Or I thought I knew. Sometimes I wasn't sure how much was my mind and how much was reality. Besides, poison is all about the dose. Everything is a little bit poisonous. Paracelsus said: "All things are poison, and nothing is without poison: the dose alone makes a thing not poison." That means there is a dose at which radiation and carbon monoxide are poison, and also a dose at which milk and ketchup and licorice are poison.

I think about this as I eat in restaurants—how everything has tiny bits of chemicals in it. I think about how those little bits keep adding up and adding up, my body filling with those chemicals.

Apple seeds have cyanide, raw honey has botulism, the air has radiation and lead. Everything has the potential to poison, but it's in knowing the dose that we find the place where we die. Rhubarb leaves are not as toxic as you might think. They are .5 percent oxalic acid. You would need to eat eleven pounds of the leaves to die.

The problem is that it can be hard to pinpoint the dose, or know the way the dose is delivered. Some things, for example, can kill you if you only touch them, some if you breathe their smoke. You cannot die from touching mushrooms, no matter how toxic they would be if eaten. You can die from touching mercury, but only over time. It's even possible to die from drinking too much water. This is called hyponatremia, and it happens when you drink so much water the salt level in your blood gets diluted and falls too low, causing your cells to swell. Of course, in medicine a little poison can be a good thing: chemotherapy, belladonna, digitalis. It's the same with the river, which can be medicine too. Sometimes at dusk I go down to the confluence, where the Susquehanna and the Swatara Creek come together. On one side, one is coming in, and on the other, the other is coming, and you can sense where they join, an inexact spot since they are continuously flowing. I get a sense of satisfaction from watching their mingling, the knitting of the smaller to the larger, and I think of them going on to join with the ocean somewhere, as if by imagining it I can float away and connect with the larger world.

# SNOW DAY

I drive to work in the snow, slowly, noticing how white the snow is, but also how it already holds within it the smallest pieces of black, so I know that by the time I drive home it will be gray slush. It all happens so quickly—newness, decay, oldness. A few times I feel the car starting to slip, moving away from my control. I was hoping that maybe the state would give us a snow day, but they didn't. They say we're emergency workers, even though we're just dealing with loans.

When I get to work, hardly anyone is there. Some of the schools are starting late, and parents are figuring out what to do with their kids. Only a few souls have made it in, and they are all gathered at the windows, talking and looking at the big snowflakes fall. The weather makes us speed up some days and slow down others, and on days when it's snowing, we all think we should lie in a warm bed and hold the one we love.

Luke is in the office already, displaying his superiority as a temp. I find him at his desk, where he is reading a book he's shown me about workplace subversion. He has put the subversive book inside the jacket of a goofy, inspirational one called *You Can Share a Cake, but Not a Cupcake,* about how teamwork can make us more productive and happy. We were all given a copy by Alissa Profit, the human resources manager, who believes she was put in her position to help people find meaning in tedious bureaucratic work, but even the pro-job people tend to laugh at the book and make jokes about it.

Since Luke and I are the only ones in my department, I sit in the break room and talk to him. I tell him I think I'm in love, and he asks, "With the old man?" and I say, "No, someone new. A woman."

He smiles and asks how old she is. When I tell him she's twenty-seven, he says that sounds more like it. I describe how Rose smells and how beautiful her hands are, but I also tell him that it's confusing being with a woman and I don't know what I'm doing.

"I know it's confusing," he says, almost whispering. "I knew that I liked boys from when I was really young. I felt horrible because of what they said about people like me in church."

"I'm sorry," I say. "I never understood that kind of religion."

"When I was young I would also speak in tongues in the church. The preacher would call anyone who could hear the words of God to come up to the pulpit and speak."

"You spoke in tongues?" It's hard to imagine. He is rational. He is philosophical, but yes, he is always trying to understand God.

"Don't laugh, but yes. It was just like sounds coming through me, and a feeling of ecstasy. But one time when I was called up, I asked God in my heart that if what I felt was wrong to strike me dead or send me a message."

"What happened?"

He'd told me about the charismatic preacher before, the man who was a combination car salesman, soap opera star, and Jimmy Swaggart. The man who could get anyone to give it up to Jesus.

"I fell to the ground. I knew that there were these words coming through me, and that they were God, but all I felt was love. It was like God was saying I love this person and this person and this person and this person and even me, the homosexual." He pauses. The look on his face is one of peace and bewilderment.

"Thanks for telling me," I whisper, because in that moment I feel like I'm in church.

"I'm seeing someone," he whispers back. His face has changed to looking like he did something bad.

"Who?"

"He's married," Luke says quickly.

"That's troubling," I say.

Luke nods. "Yeah, it's a sin, but I really like him. And after that experience, what I told you about, I don't even know if there is sin."

I think about a world with sin and a world without sin and wonder if they can both exist at the same time. Maybe in layers, I think, the world without sin under this one. For a moment, speaking in tongues, he had seen that other world.

"Where did you meet him?"

"He works here."

Luke sits at the small table. I notice on the wall a picture of a new baby with baby acne on her neck and face, wearing what looks like a tiny bridesmaid dress. Below her picture it reads, *Jesus welcomes you to the church, Holly Ann.*

I start making a pot of coffee from the coffee club. (It's a snow day— fuck the club!) Making coffee seems like a useful thing to do, even if I'm stealing it. I imagine Luke slipping off somewhere to have sex with someone at the office. For some reason it's hard for me to picture. Where do they go? How did this guy know Luke was interested in him? I don't ask who it is, but my mind flits through all of the men at the office, trying to pair them with Luke. I haven't seen him talking to anyone that much. I don't disapprove, but I don't know if the relationship will be good for Luke in the long run.

"Tell me about your girlfriend," Luke says. "What do you like about her?"

"She moves through a room in a way I like, and she drives really fast, and she talks about books and ideas."

I think how silly this sounds and how you can never explain the things that you like about someone, but Luke just listens with an under-standing half-smile.

We drink the coffee as people gradually arrive, then get to work, but all day there is the feeling of having been in a secret club together with Luke.

At 4:00, Luke walks by my desk and winks at me and puts a cookie wrapped in a napkin on my desk. He says the words, "In love," and I mouth back, *In love.* and he keeps walking.

# HANDS

I've started having fantasies about Rose's hands. Little picture's of her hands in my head at work during the day. She has such strong and slender hands, and they seem to know what they're doing. They have the sensuous feel of long-stemmed roses. They feel like lemon cakes. Like petit fours, touching me with sweetness. They feel like indecision and wanting. They feel like nothing and everything. They rip me apart. They put me together. I'm afraid of her hands, and I don't know why. They are evil and weird. Rose's hands are like floating ghosts in my imagination. I shut my eyes, and there they are, the white glow of afterimages. I'm afraid of her hands, and I don't know why. They touch me, and they make me feel. She may hate me someday, and I love her, so I hate her a little now just to be safe. I shut my eyes, and there they are, the white glow of afterimages—floating ghosts in my imagination.

# ICE

Tonight there is an ice storm, and I feel totally happy. I am at Rose's house, in her pink bed, and the sound of the frozen rain hitting the roof makes it seem like we are deep inside something. I imagine we are in a cave in the Himalayas, and we are huddling together to stay warm, and outside is a terrible storm that we can hear but that can't reach us. I imagine that I met her—the woman in the cave, who is Rose but not Rose—by chance, a beautiful Sherpa who was passing the other direction just as the storm hit, and for the night we are sheltering together.

All that matters is that we are inside and taken care of. I tell Rose I want to hide here forever and never go to work or anywhere. "What about you?" I ask.

"Well, maybe for a month," she says. "Then I want to go to the library."

"But wouldn't you like to just escape forever? Go someplace you've never been before?"

"Where would I escape to?'

"Tibet, Turkey? I don't know." I explain about the cave. Rose is lying on her stomach, and I like the line of her back. I run my hand along the curve.

"I'd like to go there, but then come back. I know it might seem weird to you, but I grew up with so much conflict that I like routine. I like being in the library. I like getting up and doing the same thing each day."

"Wanting routine does seem strange," I say. "Every day I fantasize about some way to escape my job. Sometimes I think I'll just leave at lunch and jump a train and never come back."

"You're silly. Jump a train. Come on, baby. You would miss the bed."
She tousles my hair like I'm a child.

"People still do it. They leave."

"I'm sure they do," she says. "I've always hated holidays and all of
the drama, but I like a normal day. Say it's a Wednesday, maybe, and I'm
doing my thing at the library, and some kids ask me for help. I listen to
June Groff talk about her problems, and that's okay. It's just relaxing. And
then you stop by the library, and I feel happy to see you."

I smile and slide my hand under her to touch her belly, loving the
way it's flat and soft. "I wouldn't jump a train while you're around," I say,
"unless you wanted to jump one with me."

Rose picks up a book, and I lie and watch her reading as I drift in
and out of sleep. I can hear the rain and the hail hitting the roof, and
the willow outside the window whipping its tendrils against the glass
like it's desperate to get in. I find the storm soothing. Here in bed I feel
contained, inside something, like a letter in an envelope, but there's
still a sense of separation. After we leave our mothers' bodies, we are
never really deeply inside something again. All else is a substitute. Eating is putting something inside of you, but the thing inside doesn't keep
its shape. It's funny when little kids draw things like they're still fully
themselves after they've been devoured—a whole apple just sitting in
the stomach, or Jonah sitting inside the whale. I would like to be inside
something that way, still me, but totally surrounded by something else. I
wonder if Rose feels the same when we have sex. I look at her hand lying
on the bed and think how strong her fingers are, and how she moves
them inside me. Those hands have been everywhere with her body for
as long as she has been around, and now they have been in me. I think
the need to go inside is like the need to eat. It's based on the same things.
We put our fingers and tongues and penises inside each other. But what
does it mean?

Later I lie on the bed with Rose while she cuts her toenails. I've never
watched someone do this before. It makes me feel like there is a whole
world of things I could learn by observing her. I want to watch her pee.

She won't let me, though she did let me take Polaroids of her naked breasts.

"I'm sure I'll regret that," she said.

"Never," I say. "They need to be immortalized."

"Polaroids are not immortal," she says. "I think they only last like twenty years or something."

"True, but the idea of a photo of your breasts is immortal."

"You're a sophist," she says.

"No, I'm not," I say. "What exactly is a sophist?"

"I don't know," she says. "Arguing for argument's sake, I think." She laughs. "That's you."

*game nine*

# DOLPHINS

We pretend to be dolphins in bed together. We know little about what dolphins are really like. This is a pretend game. Mostly we play and rub our shiny, slick bodies together and then we butt against the swimmers and try to make love to them with our big penises. We love swimming with people and can see inside their bodies with our sonar. This is especially entertaining, because if you think people have funny noses, they have really funny spleens.

# IMAGINARY FRIEND

Unlike most children, who lose their imaginary friends at three or four, I started seeing mine when I was seven, and I was nine when she left me. This might mean I am prone to hearing voices. Perhaps I had schizophrenia and grew out of it, or I accidentally cured myself by doing the right thing at the right time. I worry sometimes that it may return. Nobody really knows what brings on schizophrenia. Some people think it's caused by toxins, and you can cure yourself with body cleanses—by cleaning the bowels, the liver and kidneys, your dental work. I'm sure there is poison somewhere in me, but I don't know what or where it is.

So there's the possibility my imaginary friend was a hallucination, but I also have a theory that imaginary friends are aliens who visit children. Children are more open to alien visitation, and the aliens know this, and they visit them to find out about the world.

I don't know for certain if she was an alien or a ghost or a construction of my mind, but my imaginary friend was another child, what I then called an Eskimo (and now know as Inuit). The first time I saw her, it was winter. I had gone into the backyard to sled down the hill. It was a Saturday morning, and there was some snow, but not enough to attract other children.

Earlier I'd been playing inside with my stuffed animals, staging wars between different factions of them and moving the winners onto different sides of my bed. I fluctuated between loving and hating different animals, who formed a puppet theater for every drama that I could pull from my overly emotional body. This one I adored. This one was treacherous. It in fact wanted to kill this one. This new soft plush hippo was jealous of the yellow Woodstock doll without any eyes because it had such a pathetic quality of being loved to exhaustion. One week, I was devoted to a small dog that I called Pug, and the next week it was my nemesis. I projected every feeling I had onto that eight-inch brown animal with a mouselike body and large nostrils. That day, Pug had driven me to exhaustion. I couldn't stand him anymore. I saw how truly ugly and despicable he was. I went to the backyard as much to get away from Pug as to be outside.

Behind our house was a field on a hill. It was the kind of hill that children seek out in winter with their sledding eyes, waiting for the perfect amount of snow. The hill was bordered by small woods, which in my mind stretched to Black Forest dimensions. I usually played by myself, during the cold months pretending that I was alone in the Arctic. The first time I met her, I had wandered back to the woods. I saw her standing next to a holly bush. She had long black hair, and she was wearing fur boots and a fur jacket, and she looked the way I imagined someone from the Arctic would look.

I was startled by her and thought that maybe she was lost. She was sitting near the fence to the Lawrence property.

"What are you doing here?" I asked.

"I came here to see you," she said.

She was perched on her sled, eating something that looked like blackened rabbit. I was repulsed but interested.

"Why? I said. "Who are you?"

She sent me a smile and a look like she already knew my game, the kind of look that my mother shot at me when I was trying to hide something.

"We are friends," she said.

She was older than me, and though still a child, she carried herself with a sureness and steadiness. I could not imagine her standing in line for food at the cafeteria.

"I don't know you. I never saw you before," I said, thinking, *I want to know you*, but feeling cautious. I noticed she had a few freckles. Her skin looked rough, as if she were outside all of the time and the wind had blown her face into a pattern. "You don't look like anybody else here," I said.

"Guess not," she said, and was quiet. "We're still friends," she continued after a moment. "Or we could be, if you just want to."

I knew that she was perhaps not real, but I didn't care. If this was a hallucination, it was such a nice one. That's where my thinking left off, really. If had been more of a stickler for reality I would have questioned her further. Instead I thought about what she said. Nobody ever asked me to be friends so quickly before. Or not since kindergarten, at least. How easy this seemed. How much I realized I wanted this. I could be friends with this beautiful girl who seemed like she was from far away. *Yes,* I thought, *of course I want to be her friend.*

"I would like that," I said.

She held the sled pull in her hands and invited me to help her push and pull it across the woods, and she showed me a secret place where she had some meat buried in a hole in the snow. I ate some of it with her. I knew she understood things about survival that I didn't. I don't trust first-sight love now, but then I did. I was a child in love with the snow seen through her eyes.

After that day I would often go to the secret place at dusk, when most children were running home for dinner. I liked the hour when the sky first became a bright color, so that the shapes of everything were absolutely clear, and then turned purple. It is during that hour that travel between the dimensions and layers of reality is possible.

My friend taught me what moss and lichens to eat in the winter, and how to carve a nest out of the snow where you could keep warm in the coldest temperatures. She told me that the snow actually retains heat when it's packed together. She showed me how to build a structure out of sticks and leaves that you could live in, how to gather enough old crabapples, black walnuts, and grubs from the neighbors' yard to survive when you couldn't kill any elk. She taught me songs about seal hunting and told me how the seal hunter, when waiting for the seal at the breathing hole, often starts to hallucinate and see visions of seal lovers. She was a myth, the ideal of what an Inuit girl was like—part me and part everything I imagined in that cold, faraway land.

I told her about school and how everything was poison. There was poison in the snow and in the cleaning products and in the air. We would hunker in our secret place and talk for hours—about how everyone was living life so strangely, how there were all these games they were playing, like not showing someone how much you like them, and dressing in certain clothes so everyone thinks you are wonderful.

We hung out that way for two years, and then when I was nine everything changed. I suppose it crashed down on me that my fantasy would not go on forever. At that age it all became about how you looked, for girls at least, and I couldn't avoid it anymore. I was aware of the eyes that were turned on me. What mattered was what those eyes saw, not what I saw with mine.

I went out one day to talk to my imaginary friend, and she was gone. I called and called, but she didn't appear. I looked in the sky, and there was nothing.

After she left, I had an absence, a hole in me that has never filled up. I learned to swim in this hole. Sometimes the feeling of longing moved out from my body like a sweeping tentacle, searching. Winter became for me what it is for many people, a time when the exterior world matches their interior landscape of grief.

I tried to rationalize, like other people do with grief. I imagined my friend had gone on to have another life and do things on her own. I couldn't stand to think of her as a friend to other children, so I imagined her growing up and being unable to stay an imaginary friend. I imagined her becoming a Native rights lawyer.

I have continued to look for her over all these years, dreaming that she would come back to me someday. And then last night, as I slept, snow fell, covering everything without my knowledge. Usually that gives me an odd feeling of everything slipping away, but this morning I woke with the sense of having recovered something. I had the thought that

Rose is my imaginary friend. Something about Rose reminds me of her, something mysterious and yet calming. She looks at me like my imaginary friend looked at me—from a distance and yet close. She seems so near to me and yet in her own world. And when I am with her, nothing outside of us matters.

# BATH

I am drawing a bath for Rose. My apartment has an old claw-foot tub. It's the best thing about the place. I've always had this fantasy about giving someone a bath, and though Rose said it was silly, I finally convinced her. I think it will be sexy to wash her and shampoo her long hair.

I mix the bathwater, making it hot, but not too hot. I like water so hot that I can't move, but this isn't for me.

"The bath's ready," I call.

Rose comes in and takes off her pants. She is wearing silly underwear that reads Tuesday even though it's Friday.

"Have you been wearing those since Tuesday?" I ask.

She glares at me. "Do you want me to do this?"

"Yes," I say, vowing to myself to be silent and sweet.

In the bathtub she looks at me suspiciously. I run a white washcloth over her and remember the washcloths I had as a child—so worn I could see my body through them—and how I would always lay them over my breasts when I was taking a bath, even though my breasts didn't look different than the surrounding skin. I wash her breasts, which are shaped like incense cones with dark brown nipples.

"I don't like being this naked," she says.

She is lying back. and the water is making wonderful glistening drops on her shoulders.

"But you're naked all the time with me. We have sex."

"Yeah, but that's different. Here the light is so bright, and you are washing every part of me. It's weird."

"Your body is really great. I'm the one who should be embarrassed."

It's true. She is very toned, and her body looks like an athlete's, while mine is plumper, and not art-ready.

"Why?" she says.

"I'm fat."

"No, I like your body. It's juicy."

"Really?"

"Yes. Claudia, don't look at me quite so much."

"But I've never been with anyone like this before. You're my lover. I love touching you."

"Yeah, but sometimes it's just . . . too much. You don't understand distance."

"Why should I? I want to be close to you."

I feel stung by her remark. Why does she want me to be distant? Will she draw away from me further and further and disappear?

"You should go see your mother."

Rose heard my mother's voice on the answering machine this morning. I have been avoiding my mother for weeks, spending all my time with Rose. I don't want to leave Rose. Sometimes I think if I do, she won't be there when I get back, but other times I think that we will never leave each other and will grow old together and wear sweaters we knit for each other (though I don't knit yet) and sit on the porch in rocking chairs, watching the birds and weather. Why should I be reasonable? This is love.

"Don't blow off your family for me," she says.

"But I don't want to tell her about you. If she says something negative, I'll get angry."

"Then don't tell her, but see her."

I run the soap down Rose's shoulders and over her chest. Looking at Rose's breasts makes me want to suck them.

"Why don't you like me to look at you so much?" I ask.

"I don't want somebody to see everything of me," Rose says. "It's not all so great, you know."

"I want to see it all."

"Claudia, you're really sweet, but you're so young. It might get too much."

"No. It won't."

"Oh, baby," she says. "I hope you're right."

I put the shampoo on her hair, and though I make sure not to get any in her eyes, she blinks and says be careful.

# PERSONAL RADIATION

When I was a child, I had an innovative plan for dealing with nuclear waste. Each family would be given a small bottle of radiation that they'd have to hold onto and safeguard. That way it wouldn't be in the hands of the government. It would be the responsibility of the people, and you would pass it on to your grandchildren and tell them that they had to be very careful with it.

When I think about the family radiation plan now, I see it as a disaster. There would need to be constant checks to make sure everyone's bottles of radiation were safe. I used to think people would just assume responsibility. Because they would not want to hurt others, they would be wise. I had some misconceptions about history and what people were capable of, not out of evil, but simply out of carelessness. But now I see what would happen. Some people would bury their bottles in their backyards and then move away and forget to tell anybody; some would throw them in the river and let them float away; some people would hire bottle experts who would promise to safely keep their bottles for them for eternity so they could escape their civic duty; and some people would just give their bottles to their moms to take care of. It would be a toxic mess.

I would worry about my bottle constantly. I would want to just abandon it in a public place, the way unprepared mothers leave their newborns at Safe Baby Drops, but I would feel too guilty doing that. I would try to save enough money to pay someone to take care of my bottle, but then I'd worry that the professionals were corrupt and probably just dumped the bottles people gave them in Siberia or upstate New York. I would misplace my bottle and spend the day looking for it and instead find fifty pens, a Dustbuster I didn't remember buying, a drawing of me looking fat and hungry that reads, *I want a doughnut; I am bad*, and three dollars and sixteen cents in change. At the end of the afternoon, I would find the bottle in the shower and see that shampoo had leaked onto it, and I'd hope the shampoo had not penetrated the seal. I'd remember the story of Marie Curie holding the radiation in her hands, and how it killed her.

# WORK

Betty's cancer is back. She found a lump and then went in to her doctor and had the tests. She appears to be taking it well, and the women at work are going to participate in the Avon Walk for Breast Cancer. They decided this in the three days since the test results came back, which seemed way too quick to turn something horrible into something productive. I hate the way people try to make the best of death and turn it into something positive.

The despair is mirrored in the walls. Our office is painted lime green. Maybe more like lime green with a little gray in it, the type of color that you create when you decide to cook as a child and keep mixing more and more ingredients together and then add a little green food coloring to make it festive. I think about the walls at work a lot, because I don't think about work at all.

Betty is still there doing her job, leaving occasionally to get chemotherapy. She is making the best of it. I am not taking Betty's relapse so well. I have been distant and moody in the office. I feel guilty about the time I saw her at The Gingerbread Man. I could have at least forced a few pleasantries. I don't love Betty; I just don't like to think about her working here while she's dying. I think if she is dying, or is near dying, she should be on safari in Africa or climbing the Himalayas or making love with some exotic man or at least at the beach in Jamaica with her husband.

There was another storm last night, and I noticed as I left the house that the wind and ice had pulled down one of my favorite trees across the street. There are places you want to disappear into and let the mice come and find you. The tree had a space at the base of the trunk big enough to crawl into. I never did, but I imagined hiding out there with a pile of books and canned beans, just holing up there with something to read and nobody to see.

I feel my breasts over and over at night. Rose asks me what I'm doing. I tell her I'm looking for lumps. She says to only do that once a month and I'm too young to worry. I hide from her in the bathroom and check my breasts, though I don't really know what I'm doing. I've never understood those instructions about going around in circles and doing it in two minutes. I feel all kinds of things in there—mountains of things, swamps of things, deeply tangled things.

# NO MAD COW

Rose sets a plate in front of me with a hamburger and macaroni and cheese. The hamburger looks good—on a sesame bun, with some sliced tomatoes on top—but all I see is poison. Of course, Rose doesn't know that today I read an article about mad cow disease in England and how it might make the jump to the States because we're feeding cow parts to cows. I haven't really explained my poisoning fears to Rose. It seems so anti-erotic. I want her to think I am young and fun. But now I have to either eat this hamburger and worry about developing the debilitating illness that makes you go insane and then die, or find some excuse for not eating it. Rose comes out of the kitchen with ketchup and mustard.

"What do you like on your burgers?" she asks.

"Rose," I say.

"What's wrong?"

"I can't eat it. I'm sorry."

She has a look of concern on her face. I can't help thinking how the expression is beautiful, even though it's the kind of terrible thing that men say: *You look so beautiful when you're angry.* But I like that she is worried about me. When she asks how I'm feeling or touches my forehead, I feel taken care of.

"You're not a vegetarian," she says. "So what is it?"

"I'm a little afraid of the food."

"It's the poisoning thing, isn't it?"

I realize she has a name in her head for what's wrong with me, even though we've never discussed it. She noticed the books that first night we slept together, but I've always avoided talking about "the poisoning thing."

"Yes, I have a fear of poisoning," I say. I try to make it sound like a small matter, a cold, a minor irritation.

"What are you afraid of?" She sits next to me.

"Well, it comes and goes. Sometimes nothing. But sometimes botulism, E. coli, things like that."

I look at the hamburger on her plate, and I think I see small things crawling all over it, the way you can focus a microscope on something and suddenly see organisms everywhere.

"What are you afraid of now?" she asks.

I could point to the hamburger, which is dripping juices, but it seems too melodramatic. The prions never die, no heat or chemicals kill them, and they can move onto other things, so even the bun is contaminated.

"Mad cow," I say.

"Mad cow?" she says. "You mean that thing in England."

She really is unaware. She has the sense of invincibility about her, like living is her right.

"Well, they don't when it's going to hit this country," I say.

"It seems the chances are really small," she says. "But you don't have to eat it, if you're really afraid. You can have the macaroni and cheese and some salad."

"Thanks," I say, but then I think about Rose eating the hamburger. Sure, I'll live, but I'll have to watch her turning into a terrible invalid, losing her mind, and dying. I'll have to care for her, bring her water on her sickbed, and maybe they'll have to come and put a straitjacket on her—and I'll know I could have stopped it.

"Are you okay with just the mac and cheese?" she asks. "There are hot dogs in the refrigerator."

"Hot dogs," I say, a little shocked. "No, they are almost as bad. You really eat hot dogs?" I thought all people, even people not like me, knew that hot dogs were the worst parts of meat mixed together with whatever they found on the floor of the processing plant. I thought anyone who'd read *The Jungle* would never touch another hot dog.

Rose just looks at me. "Yes. I eat Philly cheesesteak too."

"Rose," I say, "I know this might seem strange." My stomach is churning, and I start to feel the same nausea I felt the night we first slept together.

"It's okay," she says. "Eat what you want."

"No," I say. "It's not just that. I mean, I don't think I can watch you eating the burger. You know that they feed cows to cows in this country. It's a kind of cannibalism and will lead to mad cow. If not now, eventually." *Please, God,* I pray to myself, *do not let her eat it.*

"You don't want me to eat it," she says, "but I eat burgers other times when you're not around, and I'm really not scared. Besides, I want to eat it. I like hamburgers."

My bowels are cramping with terror. I think of possible ways to avert what's about to happen. I could steal the hamburger and run out of the house, or I could spill my drink on it and make it too soggy to eat. I usually let other people eat whatever they want. I even watch my mother eat things that might kill her, but with Rose, I just really don't want her to die, ever.

"I'm sorry," I say. "I just can't stand to think about you eating it. I'll take you out for dinner. We can go to Nippy's. You haven't had the oyster pie yet."

"Oyster pie is okay? That sounds like a stomach ache to me," she says with irritation.

"Well, it won't kill you," I say.

"You mean you really are worried that if I eat this, I'll die?"

"Yes," I say. Now I am almost desperate. I would beg her not to eat it, if I thought it would help. But you can't beg with Rose.

"How often do you get like this?" she asks.

"From time to time," I say. "But only with what I eat. I usually don't care what other people eat. If it makes you feel any better, I think it's because I care about you so much that it's spreading to you."

Her troubled look gives me a terrible feeling.

"Claudia, I can't let your worries control my life," she says. "Tonight we'll go out for oyster pie, but maybe you could find someone, a therapist or someone, to talk to about this. You don't want fear to rule you, baby."

She says this without irony, though her tone is like that of a cheesy self-help book. I am relieved for the moment, but I know there will be other times when she won't listen to me, and I will have to watch her eating poison, then stay up all night worrying she's going to die. I don't want fear to rule my life, but it's not so simple. I want my mind to be good, but it's bad, just so bad.

# WARNING

A problem I worry about is how we are going to mark all the toxic dump sites so people in the future know where they are. What if it's a thousand years from now, and the half-life of the radiation is still twenty-one thousand years, and people don't know English or understand our symbols? I read about a team of researchers who are trying to create a universal warning symbol. They are having a hard time figuring one out. How do you convey danger without it seeming exciting? Something that's meant to be frightening and indicates *stay away*, like the image of a skull and crossbones, might make people think there is something really cool there. The warnings on pharaohs' tombs just caused lots of people in funny hats and tan clothes to try and find something to loot. Anything that warns someone off could just as easily encourage them to find out what you are trying to hide. Warnings are only fuel for the imagination.

# OUR DARK TIME

There are ten messages from my mother on my answering machine. I can't erase them, and I can't call. It's hard to explain why. I just know that if I call I will become extremely depressed.

After my father disappeared, my mother stopped leaving the house. I remember it as the worst winter ever, bleak, with ice storms and ten-foot drifts of snow. My mother stayed home and cried. Nobody cleaned, and the house grew musty and smelly. We would forget to take the trash out, and it would pile up on the back porch. We didn't shovel our walk. The city sent us citations, and my mother threw them in the trash with the TV dinner tins. She asked me to come straight home after school. When I did, she would be in bed with the TV on. We would lie there and watch after-school specials and the news and sitcoms. Sometimes I would read next to her, *Jane Eyre* or *Heart of Darkness* or *The Bell Jar*, while she watched her shows. We rarely talked, but I liked the close warmth of her body. At 6:00 she would go and put the TV dinners in the toaster oven, maybe Salisbury steak or lasagna, and then bring them back to the bed. I didn't do my homework. Around 11:00 I fell asleep during the late news, and then I would wake up in the morning and get ready for school while she watched the morning shows. I never knew where my father had gone or if he was coming back. When I started to ask my mother, she got angry, so I stopped bringing it up.

There was another reason I never asked, a secret reason, a fear that was building inside of me and would grow larger.

That was the time of our depression. The time when we didn't talk to people. The time when we became each other's best friend.

After a few months, my mother found a new job. She started leaving the house again, though she still didn't like to be alone after work. She didn't want me to be in clubs or the school play. I came straight home from school and read books.

If I call my mother, if I see her, I'll either tell her about Rose or I won't. If I don't, then I'll be lying and cutting myself off from her. I know she wouldn't understand this, but I have a feeling if I pick up the phone, things will change. I don't want anyone to do or say anything that will make me feel bad about what I have with Rose. I don't ever want to feel the way my mother did after my father was gone.

# BAR

Rose and I go out to a bar called Brett's Place, which is dark and kind of ratty inside and has NASCAR posters on the walls. It's mostly filled with locals, good old boys and nice neighborly girls, people in their twenties with kids and mortgages, and a few regulars who are there every night.

Tonight they are playing bad music on the jukebox. There is a long wooden bar with ornate decorations, and the bartender looks like all the men do here at a certain age—balding and with a beer belly, yet his smile having gotten sweeter with time. And I am drinking some sickly sugary hard lemonade. Rose turns her nose up at this and drinks beer, local beer. She has developed a taste for Yuengling Black & Tan, which is made in Pennsylvania, up in coal country, and she feels makes her fit in. She doesn't know that she will never fit in, that it would be nearly impossible for someone like her to fit in here, unless she hid an awful lot of herself. Or maybe I'm wrong. Maybe I'm just odd.

We spend twenty minutes looking at the songs on the jukebox and talking about what we want to hear, and then Rose chooses Patsy Cline's "Crazy," and we ooze into our seats and pretend we are somewhere else or that *here* is just on the edge of things. Since Rose has come along, Riverton doesn't seem so boring. She has awakened me to everything in the town in a new way. I see the old houses that she notices and the plaques about historical events, even an old ferry house from the early nineteenth century.

Up at the bar, I see Tommy Conroy, who I went to fifth grade with, and he gives me a look like he knows that I am *with* Rose and not just with Rose. We try to keep it cool, but I put my arm around her to spite him.

We're having a conversation about the nature of love, and I ask her how many times she's been in love. She looks at the ceiling for a moment before turning back to me.

"Five," she says.

"Five. My God."

I feel slightly ill. That's one complete hand of fingers. Five people with different parents (ten parents) and all of their sexual history and their weird differences and fucked-upness and all of the places they like to be touched and don't like to be touched. Thinking all of that feels like looking at a map of the universe. Holding body maps with special places of five people in your head. It seems infinite to me. But that's the number of people she has loved, not how many she's had sex with. I can't even ask her that.

Lately I've been fretting that Rose is going to meet somebody else and leave me. The fear seems to arise from my belief that Rose will never love me as much as I love her. To her I'm just another woman in a long history of women, but she is my first love. Before her, nothing felt like this. Without her, everything will go back to being dull. I have another drink. I try to smile.

"You mean five all the way in love, genuine love."

"Yeah, whatever love meant to me at the moment. Five where I couldn't think of anybody else and I imagined I would be with that person forever, if we didn't kill each other first. Really, most of them were kind of crazy. I guess I was too, then. I've gotten better at picking," she says and smiles at me.

"Who was your first?" I ask. I want to know, but I don't. I can't help comparing myself to other women Rose has been with—wilder women, prettier women, women who were 100 percent lesbians.

"My first girlfriend," Rose says, "was the daughter of this really rich family. We were so crazy for each other. We were going to run away together. She had been to Europe with her family, and she said that we could go to Paris and find jobs off the books working in a café. She used to pick me up in her convertible, and we would go out, but once we stayed out all night and her parents called the police. The cops found the car because we were parked in a city park having sex. Her parents thought she was out all night with a guy."

My mind races as Rose talks—how easily she has tumbled into love. All of her experiences are frightening to me.

"The police officer told her father that he found his daughter, and they didn't have to worry about her being pregnant. We laughed about that so hard, but she never saw me again. I was completely broken-hearted. Man, I cried and would drive by her house and call her name, and nothing. *Je t'aime, je t'aime*, and she cut me off like that."

Rose seems happy talking about the sorrow. She is on her third Yuengling and relaxing in her seat, looking a little devilish.

I slide from the booth to get more drinks at the bar, and I see Mike Singer, the boy whose mother had the affair with my father, but he's not a boy now. He's tall and has nice wavy black hair, and he's wearing slightly dirty clothes like he just came from some job where he used his body. I'm suddenly anxious that he'll see me and say something, so I look away as I get our drinks and take them back to the table. As Rose and I sip, I steal a glance at Mike, hoping he doesn't recognize me. I'd heard he went away to college and never came back, but he's here. His confidence seems to have increased from high school. He's talking with some other people his age, leaning against the bar, relaxed. If he recognized me, would he say something? If he did, what would it be? I imagine him coming over to throw a note on the table. I can't stand that we share this sense of humiliation.

"Let's go," I say to Rose.

"Why, we're having fun." Rose senses that something has changed. "Did someone come in that you know?"

"Not really."

"An old boyfriend?"

"No."

Mike is laughing at something someone has said. Why does other people's laughter always sound louder than our own?

"Somebody from childhood," I say. "He knows something embarrassing about me." Saying it, I think, *Why is it about me? It's about my father.*

"God, you look sick. It must be something bad." Rose looks concerned.

"No, no, it's just my father. He was an asshole."

"Do you wanna tell me about it?"

Rose runs her fingers along my neck in a soothing gesture. She is trying to meet my eyes, but I stare at the table.

"No," I say. "Please, let's just go home."

She slides from the booth, but as she does, she says, "You can't shut me out like this. You need to tell me what's going on."

We are almost at the door when Mike sees me.

"Claudia Hecht," he says. "How are you?"

From his light tone he seems to have forgotten everything that we meant to each other. Perhaps that day in the cafeteria is just another memory for him. I suppose his mother didn't disappear after it happened, and maybe there were many men and many times like that for him.

"Hi, Mike," I say. "Good to see you."

My voice betrays that it does not feel at all good to see him. Recognition and pain cross over his face, as if he's empathetically picked up on my emotions—or is he reliving that day too?

"Good to see you too," he says. "You look good." He looks into my eyes for a second, and I can see that he knows what I'm thinking and is trying to reach out. I don't want to go there. I turn away and push through the door.

We walk home, and I don't hold Rose's hand. The night is a dizziness; there might be an opening behind any turn that pulls me into the past. It's thick and dark and reminds me of lying in my childhood bedroom at night, thinking I saw bats flying toward my window. If I step in the wrong place, a manhole might open, and I'll fall back into that bed, with only thin walls separating me and my parents. My father, who is drunk, is rambling on about crazy things—a business he wanted to start and how my mother stopped him, how stupid he is, how stupid she is, something about her voice that he can't stand, and my mother is whispering, her tone calming. But he isn't calmed, and the exchange turns suddenly, and he is shouting now, and there is the sound of his hand hitting her and her crying. He never hit me, but my mother wore the pathetic pancake makeup of shame to work too many times.

In bed Rose puts her arms around me. "Don't be afraid of the past," she says. She touches my hair, and it feels so sweet. "I've been afraid of the past for a long time," she says, "but it really can't get you. It's gone. Not here anymore. Like the Buddhists say, it doesn't exist."

I hug Rose even as I think she doesn't understand. She wants me to be something I'm not. *Maybe I'm not as brave as you,* I think. *Maybe I can't fight all my demons and get a job I like and become a librarian and have oodles of women lovers and be strong and beautiful. Maybe I just need to hide.*

# FLOODING

It's Rose's day off, but I go to the library anyway, looking for Hal. I want
to take him up on the friend offer. When I first met Rose, she seemed
like the easiest person in the world to talk to—I could say anything—but
now I worry if I bring up my poisoning fear, she'll think I'm trying to
control her or that I'm being needy. I feel like I have to watch what I say
with her or she'll think I'm crazy. It's become clear that I am a thousand
times more messed up than Rose is, and if I show her how messed up,
she'll leave. I've decided to try to get over my obsession with poisons.
There must be some way of cutting out that part of my brain. I'm hoping Hal can help, but I'm nervous. I have this pressing need to blurt out
what's wrong. If I don't, I may never talk about it.

Hal is shelving books. He looks happy to see me.

"Hey there, kiddo," he says. "How are you?"

"Can I talk to you?" I say. My jeans suddenly feel too tight, my stomach rubbing against the button just under my navel.

Hal smiles warmly as if nothing bad had happened between us, as if
just yesterday we hung out together. "Sure," he says. "Wanna get a cup
of coffee?"

Hal's a volunteer, so he can take a break whenever he wants. We walk
to a Hardee's up the block. It's the closest place. We each get cups of bad
coffee, and Hal offers to pay for mine. They have the kind of creamer
that doesn't need to be refrigerated, which I've never been able to figure
out. Milk goes bad, so this must be some concoction of plastic ingredients. Things that never decay worry me; it's natural to rot.

I drink my coffee with just sugar, but Hal empties three of the little
poison vessels into his. We sit at the window. It's not the most picturesque

view. There's a row of old houses with peeling paint and cheap aluminum siding and a dog chained to a post in one of the yards and some old
rowboats and lumber in a pile a rat would love.

"Remember when I talked to you about my fears?" I say.

Hal nods. "Your fears of dying by being poisoned?"

"Yes. I know they're crazy. And you said that I should just not be
afraid of dying."

What else did he say? I can't really remember. All I remember was
feeling like none of it would work for me.

"Well, I said that might be one technique." Hal looks at me with
concern. "Are you okay?"

"It's gotten worse," I say. "Now I'm afraid of Rose being poisoned. I
really like Rose, and maybe I love her, and I'm afraid I'm going to ruin
this thing we have. But I've started worrying about her dying. I can't
stand to see her eat things like beef."

"Well, I'm not a therapist, Claudia, and maybe you should see one, but
after you talked to me about your fear, I did read some on the subject."

The idea of Hal reading up on my problem and trying to help me gives
me a warm feeling. That seems like another idea of love, someone doing
research for you. I look at him across from me, his kind blue eyes and
his creased face. I see now that he is an old man with wrinkles. I don't
feel the same way about him that I do about Rose, who inspires a lust
that leaves me confused and hungry. He gives me a sense of being taken
care of, but even though he wants to help me, I don't know if he can.
I'm too crazy in the head.

"There is something wrong with me," I say. "It's getting on Rose's
nerves."

"I read about a technique called flooding that might help you," Hal says.

"Flooding. What's that?"

At the next table some teenagers are talking loudly about giving hick-
ies. I notice a beautiful, awful love bite on one guy's neck, the kind of
thing that would make me ashamed. He's showing it proudly to the other
guys. I think about giving Rose a hickey, maybe somewhere hidden, like
the skin above her breast.

"It's a process of trying to overcome an irrational fear by overloading the system with the fear. For example, if you were afraid of snakes, we would set up a situation where there were snakes all around you. Your system would be flooded by the fear for the moment, but it would build up a tolerance to the fear and you wouldn't feel it as much."

"Hal, that kind of sounds horrible. I mean, wouldn't being surrounded by the fearful stuff make the person with the fear feel even more fear?"

"Yes, initially. That's why it's called flooding. You are overwhelmed by the feeling, but after a while your system realizes that it can go through the fear and survive it."

"Maybe I should just think about death, like you said before."

"Claudia," Hal says softly, "if you really want to work on this, you could see a therapist."

"No, I don't want to do that. You're just as good. I know it. I trust you. I don't want to talk to a stranger. I know they are knowledgeable, but a smart stranger is still a stranger." There is an axe hanging over my head. How do I explain that if I see a therapist, they might find something really wrong with me, a way my brain is broken and can never be fixed. I sigh. "So how would I flood myself for my problem?"

"A therapist would help," he says, "but if you want to try flooding, you could surround yourself with poisons, I guess, and maybe eat things that are a little bit poisonous."

There is a strong afternoon light falling on Hal's face, bringing out the highlights and shadows. He looks like the wise old man in some black-and-white movie.

"Eat poisonous things. Are you serious?"

The coffee tastes horrible, and I feel itchy. I look at the little cup of nondairy creamer in my hand, and I realize I have unconsciously put it in my coffee. My God, I'm doing it already.

"Well, not arsenic or anything, but what's something mildly poisonous? Maybe food past its expiration point or moldy bread or raw honey. They say raw honey has a tiny bit of botulism in it, so you shouldn't feed it to babies."

"I know about raw honey," I say. "I know about botulism. I know about dented cans and the problem with Inuit people getting it from beached whales. You want me to eat botulism?" I feel slightly dizzy.

"Not enough to kill you or even make you sick," Hal says calmly.

"Just enough to poison me a little?"

Hal gaze is steady, gentle. All around us people are eating hamburgers, and they are not at all afraid of dying.

"Enough to make you see that you aren't going to poison yourself. In homeopathic medicine, you give yourself a little bit of the poison to cure yourself."

"Is this something you read in some book on the occult? If I try this, it's going to make me crazy. I don't think I'll ever sleep."

I look around to see if anyone is listening to our conversation. The man and woman next to us seem to be angry about something, and there is a woman with some kids who looks too tired to care.

"No, it's modern therapy. Well, it might not be the right thing for you. I don't know. Why don't you just try a little? Maybe there is something here you are afraid of."

Of course, I could eat a hamburger. We're sitting in a hamburger joint surrounded by meat that may have mad cow, but there is no way I'm going to go there. I don't even feel that's an irrational fear. That's a rational fear. I can't start with the hamburgers. "I don't like dirty food," I say.

At the table next to us, the tired woman is trying to get her three children to stop arguing about French fries. The big kid, who looks like a bully if I ever saw one, with hefty legs and arms, steals some fries from the little kid, who then whines loudly, "Mom, Joey stole my fries." I don't know which one is more annoying, the bully or the whiner. Probably she doesn't either.

"What if we dropped something on the floor, and then you ate it?" Hal says.

"Drop something on the floor? Here? Now? You want me to eat something that's been on the floor? That's disgusting."

Again I look around. The colors in Hardee's were chosen with optimal disgust in mind—brown and orange. The floor looks like it hasn't been mopped in days, and it is littered with soda lids, plastic straws, and napkins here and there amid the general dirt and spilled food.

"Well, it won't kill you."

"But there is E. coli on people's shoes, and dog shit, and probably heavy metals in the dirt, and . . . I don't know, all kinds of chemicals."

"If we dropped something on the floor just for a second, it wouldn't have that much of the dirt on it. I'd eat it, too. I do all the time at home."

"What do you want to drop?"

"What about a biscuit?"

Biscuits are kind of hard. Maybe it wouldn't pick up too much bad stuff. If this flooding will really work, then it might be worth it. If I can scare my body into forgetting about this whole poisoning thing, Rose wouldn't look at me sometimes like I'm some kind of a special case.

"Okay, a biscuit," I say.

Hal goes to the counter and comes back. He unwraps the biscuits.

"I got the kind without gravy," he says, "so it wouldn't pick up too much dirt."

He takes one of the biscuits and drops it on the floor under the table, counts to five, and then picks it up. The floor is gray. I see some gum on it, straw wrappers, and a half-exploded ketchup packet. He takes the other biscuit, drops it on the floor, counts to five, and then picks it up.

"You can have your choice," he says.

The biscuits are spinning when I look at them. *Just do it,* I think. I take the biscuit nearest me. It doesn't have any visible dirt on it, maybe a hair. There is a hair on it. I flick the hair off. Hal has already picked up his biscuit, spread some butter on it, and started eating. I'm still staring at mine.

"It tastes good," Hal says, smiling as he chews.

I pick up my biscuit. *This is for love,* I think, *for love, for love.* I shut my eyes and take a bite.

# PORN

After work, I go to Rose's house. I've been going there almost every day lately, and it's blurry and wonderful and sometimes frightening to spend so much time with someone. I feel seen by her, and yet sometimes I still want to hide. Where does it come from—this longing to be both visible and invisible? I don't even feel like I'm the same person anymore.

When I get to her house, Rose is making some spaghetti and clams. I walk up to her and smell her neck.

"Wanna watch a porn movie?" she asks.

"I don't know. I never watched one."

She laughs at me. "You're cute," she says. "Such an innocent."

*I'm not in the least innocent*, I think, but what does it matter? You can't prove that to someone if they think otherwise. It's one of those non-provable things, like trying to persuade someone you're sexy. They either see it or they don't.

"This is an old one," she says. "It's not so bad. It's kind of funny."

When dinner is simmering, she turns on the movie. It shows two women in an apartment. One of the women has frosted blonde hair, and the other has short black hair. They are having sex on a beanbag chair in an apartment that looks like it has very few furnishings. Everything is white in the apartment: white couch, white chair, white carpeting, white walls. The lighting seems horrible—the stark glare of fluorescents in an office building. They move from the beanbag to the kitchen and look in the refrigerator (white) and find a carrot and start using it to have sex.

I like the woman with the short black hair. She looks kind of wild, the way I think I'd like to be. She has medium-sized breasts, and they don't look fake. The other woman looks more like you would think a porn star should, with large breasts and dyed hair. I feel kind of turned on but also a little disgusted by the movie. It all seems so fake: the set, the dialogue, the horrible lighting.

Still, it's hypnotic watching them and how they keep fucking in different ways, with a dildo, their hands, and then the carrot—and how it all seems to make them so happy, and they keep doing it, and there is an energy there that seems unnatural. They are not taking breaks or having small conversations or taking naps in between; it's just this extraordinary enthusiasm for endless sex. I want to see them doing something else for a moment, maybe making bread or getting the mail. I am lost. Rose strokes my arm; I stiffen.

"What do you think they are thinking about?" I ask.

"I don't know," she says. "What are you thinking about?"

She runs her hand over my hair. Does she want to have sex while we watch this? Could I do that?

"Do you think they're in love?" I ask.

"No. Maybe they feel lust, or maybe they are just doing it for the camera. It doesn't matter. It's just sex."

"I don't understand how you can have sex with someone you don't feel anything for," I say.

Rose laughs. "It's not so hard. I could have sex with you even if I didn't feel anything for you. I mean, I do feel a lot for you, but if we just met in a bar I'd have sex with you just based on how cute you are."

"Like you've done with so many other women," I say.

"Not that many," she says, smiling, "but yeah, some . . . some."

"That's disturbing to think about," I say. She probably thinks I'm being prudish. Last month the idea wouldn't have bothered me, but now I don't want to think about Rose with other women. Love has poisoned me with jealousy.

Rose looks at me, surprised. "Why would that bother you?" she asks. "I like your body. I like your face. Not everything is about emotions."

"It's like thinking about my body without me in it."

Rose kisses my ear. "You're funny," she says.

I am not turned on. I feel like Rose has in some way betrayed me—that she could take my insides out and put something else in there and it would still be okay.

"I don't want to fool around," I say. It's after dinner time, and we have forgotten to eat, and my stomach is turning.

"Are you upset by the porn?" she asks, her expression grave, like a nurse's.

"No, I'm upset by you liking it so much." I'm upset by how little experience I have, and how she is going to leave me for a sexier woman who can not only do all of those things in the movie but can also let her eat hamburgers.

"Okay," she says. "Let's do something else."

We eat, then afterward go into separate rooms and read books, like an old married couple. Later, when I go to bed with her, she is touching me and trying to warm me up.

"I don't want to play porn people," I say. "I mean, you are you."

She looks at me flatly, unblinking. "Sure, "she says, "I'm me, but you pretend all of the time, like I'm an alien or some kind of weird fantasy?"

"Yeah, but that's different. It's not dirty."

"What's dirty?" She laughs. She is making me uncomfortable, as if I'm some kind of freak for feeling this way.

"I don't know. The porn movies just seem soulless to me."

"And aliens aren't?"

"I have deep feelings for aliens," I say.

"That's nice," she says. "I'm fine with that. But maybe it's not always about your fantasy," she says. "Other people can have them too."

I hear the hurt in her voice as she turns from me. "I'm okay with you having fantasies. Just not some generic thing," I say. "What do you want me to be?"

"I don't know what I want you to be," she says and turns out the light and doesn't touch me again.

# ALL MY PRETTY ONES

I have a habit of imagining the deaths of my loved ones, but it's hard with Rose. She seems so strong and eternal. There is something about her that's separate, that makes me feel I'm not touching her all the way. She seems impervious on some level. When I think of her dead, it's not from poison or a disease. The only way I can imagine it is by some freak accident of nature. I see her climbing a mountain, then an avalanche covering her. And because of the snow and ice, her body doesn't really decay. She lies there looking beautiful, like a snow princess. Of course, I don't want her to die, and I know it's morbid to think about, but I have this habit of picturing everyone I love as dead. It's a rehearsal that I run through in my mind, to make the shock less when death actually happens.

Other people can just go through life not thinking much about death, and it's good not to think about it, but for me it's always popping up in the back of things. Even sex makes me think of death, because when I am close to a person all I can think of is that they will die someday and how they will die.

For Hal I picture a heart attack, and I am standing there not knowing what to do. I run looking for a reference book like *What to Do in an Emergency*. I feel the limits of books because it's too late to look things up. There is guilt that I could have done more, that I should be a person who does things instead of spending so much time with books.

My mother I see dying in a slow way, and I'm there with her at the end and have a soft conversation with her. This is the only way I can imagine it happening.

My own death I picture over and over, but it happens differently: the food poisoning, the gradual decline from exposure to secret toxins, a bad blood transfer, carbon monoxide leaking into my apartment. It happens, but I don't have an image of what my body would look like. I don't know what would be gone. Everything? Or would there still be something of me left over after I'm dead?

When Rose gets up early to take a run, I play the porn movie. I feel guilty playing it after telling her it disgusted me, but I'm trying to figure out something in it. One woman has the other pushed up against a wall and is fucking her with a strap-on dildo. The other one's hair is getting smashed by the wall, and the woman fucking her moves her hair down, smoothing it out. Other than that, they fuck and smile with lipsticked mouths and look very pretty. It is the hair smoothing that gets to me. It's a small moment that seems lost amid all of the fucking and sucking but indicates some kind of awareness outside of the context of the film. I don't know what I want from a woman. I don't know if I want her to smooth my hair or fuck me or both.

Being by myself in Rose's house makes me feel lonely. I've never been so immersed in a person before. Even in my apartment there is her presence—some of her things lying around, her smell on everything. Sometimes it feels like an invasion. I read the books she brings home from the library, eat her food, watch her porn. She is taking up so much space in my head that I'm not sure there's room in there for me.

Because of this, I am gradually beginning to think of myself as something separate from the world. A part of me is floating out somewhere else, and I can't just grab that part and bring it along with the rest of me. Sometimes I worry I can't really be close to anyone. I think I want this great intimacy, but I also resist it. I look around at the photos in Rose's living room. Some of the people in them she has told me about, but there are many strangers. Rose is smiling and laughing with the strangers, and sometimes she has expressions I've never seen. If I've never seen her look like this, how could I really know her?

*game ten*

# PRISON

I have been taken to a city I don't know and imprisoned for a crime I didn't commit, or one I did commit but that shouldn't be a crime. The prison smells like shit, though occasionally the scent of lemons comes through the open vents high above our heads. Somehow, they allow lemon trees to be grown nearby. I hear carts outside, people selling things, and sometimes automobiles zooming by and voices fighting in a foreign language. I was never good with other languages. I am a prisoner because I chose to speak the way I wanted. It has become against the law to use metaphors and similes. I did it anyway. Just a few similes for my lover.

I wear a gray dress. No one touches me. I numb my mind by pushing my legs together and masturbating sitting there in my cell.

You are a guard inside the prison. I can tell you are in love with me. You watch me when I get dressed. You bring a brush for my hair. You wear a stiff-looking dress, and your hair is cut short like a man's, and you are crazy for me.

One night I wait for you. For a long time, you don't come. I listen to the sounds in the prison. I can hear the breathing of all these women. I try to hear people's individual breathing. I try to make my ear into an amplifier and hear every breath of every woman. Even though I hate most of them, I am reminded when they sleep of warm animals—soft and human. I don't talk to people here. I am afraid whatever is unique in me will be taken away. Here, if people see the smallest thing to steal, they will steal it. They will steal my ideas, my passion. They will steal my love. I show them nothing. They think I am steely hearted. Perhaps I am. Perhaps all of the faking will make me really cold. I write poems in my head and memorize them. I remember the story of Osip Mandelstam, how he had to keep his poetry in his head while he was in Stalin's gulag, and then he would tell his wife, and she kept his poetry in her head for many years, and that was the way it survived.

Finally, late at night—morning really—you come to my cell. You ask where I'm from. You ask me the details of my crime. You want me to repeat the metaphors and similes I used. I say, *It's a crime*. You say, *No, you're just confessing*. I say that I told my lover she was like the salt of the sea on my skin. *Really,* you say. *How horrible.* I tell you she tasted like a peach that has been sitting in the sun all day. *My God,* you say. *How decadent.* I tell you that when she kissed me it felt like the moon sinking to the bottom of a mountain lake. You enjoy hearing my crimes. You say, *Make up more.* I say, *I can't. It's illegal.* What I mean is that you are not worthy of my similes yet.

You make love to me. You lick me; you eat me. I don't resist. Why should I? You are like a ray of light in a black room. You are like a fresh oyster in a fast-food restaurant. You tell me I taste like honey, that I smell like the first blade of grass in the spring. The blush on the top of my breasts is crushed raspberries. You are speaking the most forbidden things. I say, *Are you mad? What if they hear? I don't care,* you say. *The world is so drab. It has no color. It is a gray classroom in winter. Yes,* I say, *the world has the taste of a bad TV dinner. Yes,* you say, *we used to know that the world could be so many things. Now it must be what it is, and it can't even be that anymore.* You tell me I am a fox, a kumquat, the galaxy colliding with a new sun. *Yes,* I say. *Yes, yes.*

# FLOODING HOMEWORK

I've decided not to tell Rose about flooding. I'm afraid she'll get too excited about it and want to flood me too much at once, like with hamburger or raw honey. After the exercise with Hal in Hardee's, I've been trying to gradually flood myself. I've made a list of mild flooding foods, and I'm trying to eat them. I've done three things on my list already.

1.  Bread with visible mold on it. Ate from my refrigerator this week. It was green. It didn't make me sick. √

2.  Home-canned food. Ate some jelly that Fran had canned herself. Felt extreme fear afterward, but went back the next day for more. It's actually really good (strawberry). Fran says she will teach me to can my own. I feel a sense of panic at this idea, but I am working on accepting it. √

3.  Hot dog bought off the street. I'm working up the courage. There is a man near work who sells hot dogs from one of those metal carts. I've always questioned the cleanliness of the whole thing, plus hot dogs are disgusting.

4.  Food from a dented can. I went to a bargain store and intentionally bought a dented can, but I will never eat what's in it. There are reasonable risks and unreasonable risks, and I think this one is unreasonable.

5.  Eggs sunny-side up. (There is a risk of salmonella.) I have started ordering my eggs this way when I eat out. This is one of the easiest flooding exercises for me, I think because I like saying *Sunny-*

*side up, please.* It sounds happy coming out of my mouth, and the sweet, motherly waitress who works at the diner doesn't seem like she could kill me (even though I know poisoners come in all forms). √

# HUNGER

In the far north country, where if you are outside for ten minutes without a fur on you will freeze to death and men supposedly wife-swap as a matter of custom, there is a concrete reason for bodily closeness.

But not here. It's hot. Summer has snuck up on me, and it's been in the low nineties for the past few days.

Rose and I go swimming at the town pool. The water is jammed body to body with all of Riverton—friends and neighbors and enemies. I see some people I know, and I smile but try not to get them talking. The beautiful Laura Brody is there, but I can hardly believe it's her. The homecoming queen is pregnant, with a huge belly. She looks so normal. I even see her changing into her bathing suit in the locker room, an act of vulnerability that would seem beneath her, especially in her large state. I can't help but peek at her body. She's still pretty, but with a cool-looking belly and stretch marks. Could she have become human?

I am with Rose, and she is my lover, and that makes me special. My mind is swarming, moving, exiting this world and going into another. Like a little starfish in the deep, unknown sea. I wanted what I wanted, and the sea entered into me and I entered into the sea. I swim in the water and I go under and do flips and I start flipping forward with my eyes closed and I do ten flips without breathing, one after the other, quick, my body moving almost without my control. When I finish, Rose swims up next to me, looks me in the eyes for a beat, and says, "Lets have a tea party." I used to have tea parties as a child, where I would go to the bottom of the pool and sit and pretend to drink tea with a friend, but when Rose and I get to the bottom, she reaches over and puts her hand under the top of my suit for a second, and her fingers just brush the edge of my nipple, and she looks at me under the water, a look that burns a hole in my skin. We're under the water and nobody knows what we're doing and nobody suspects that while they are living their boring lives, we are having this, this, this.

At home, I lie on the bed in my suit, still a little wet.

Rose comes and touches my breasts and belly. "You're cold," she says. "Your body feels like a fish."

"Warm me up."

"Is that all you ever want—warm me up, touch me, fuck me?" She smiles.

"I am unrepentant," I say.

"You're a greedy one," she says and takes off my swimsuit top.

"Greedy for you."

"Oh, sure, me, it's all about me."

Her mouth feels so warm on my cold breasts. I think back to our conversation about the porn film, and I feel cold inside too. She runs her hands over my body, making my flesh warm. My hair is still a little wet, and she slicks it back.

"You look good this way."

She spreads her body on top of mine. She is sucking my breasts, and I am spreading my legs and rubbing against her thigh. I kiss her back and her ear and pull her earlobes into my mouth.

She cups me under the head with her hand and turns my face to her. I see the redness in her cheeks, and her eyes, which are hard to read. I am not ready for her; she is going too fast, but she pushes me along. I have this emotional side that wants to take things slow, but she makes me want more. She is in control of me.

"Is this is what you want, greedy baby?" she asks as she pulls down my bikini bottoms.

I feel her finger going inside of me, and it feels good moving into me, and I know it's her finger and has been on her hand all day and more days and even days before I was born and it's a part of her and that makes me want it, to have my smell on her after she leaves. To have her sweet smell on me.

She opens her hand, and I feel this inside of me. It hurts a little, but in a good way. Her other arm is pinning me down. "Do you want this?" "Yes," I say. "Tell me that you want this." "Yes, I want this." Her eyes are black in the light, and I can't see into them at all. They are like shallow wells with a terrible piercing quality. She captures me there. And she can see me wanting this. She likes to see it in my face. And even though I'm happy, I feel a sense of dread. I can never just relax and be content, because people can always change their minds.

I know that Rose will leave me, and I will be alone again.

# GIRL IN THE WELL

I wake up and feel a weight on my chest, a sinking. I've had the dream about the well again. In the dream, I am kneeling next to an old well, and I hear crying. There is a girl down there. I throw her a rope, but she says she is lodged in between things and can't get out. There is nothing I can do. I start to go and get the police, but she says she doesn't want me to leave. She wants to talk.

Rose is sleeping, and I almost shake her awake so she can comfort me, but I'm afraid she'll be upset if I do. She looks a little like a stranger lying there. How long have I even known her? Eight months. How could I have let myself fall so blindly in love with someone I have known for so short a time? She'll deceive me. She'll leave me. She has other plans and such wild women in her past and future. My heart is beating fast. I remember what I had for dinner and wonder if there is any chance I've poisoned myself. Spaghetti and tomato sauce. No, those are okay. I go to the kitchen and get some orange juice.

The juice feels like acid on my tongue, too sharp. I sit in the living room and drink my acid. I think about the little girl in the well, how we were having a conversation about her favorite book. I felt a terror that there was no way for me to help her, that I should be doing something, calling the police, running somewhere, but she was begging me to stay, and I felt caught. I think about Hal saying that everyone in your dream is you. I notice a figure in the hallway. It's Rose. She looks sleepy and pretty, wearing boxer shorts and a white t-shirt, her loose hair falling over her face.

"What are you doing up?" she asks.

"I'm sorry. I dreamt that a little girl fell down a well."

I'm on the couch with my legs bent, holding my knees close to me like a child.

"That sounds terrible. Is something bothering you?"

Rose doesn't like to talk about dreams much. She says they are caused by anxiety in daily life.

"What are you scared of?" she asks.

She always wants to figure things out. She wants solutions and answers and for things to be simple. I wish she would ask me about my dream so I could tell her about the girl, how nice her voice sounded as she told me about her favorite book, which was the story about the seven brothers swallowing the sea.

"I guess I'm scared of losing you, of fucking up." As I say this, I worry that I am doing that very thing at this very moment. By speaking my fear, I'm ruining what's between us.

"Don't say that." Rose turns her face away.

"Why?" I say. Why can't I say what I think? Why do I need to hide my fears from her, hide what I'm really thinking?

Rose sits on a chair across the room. "When people start talking that way, it means they really want to break up," she says.

"Because I'm afraid of you leaving me, it means I want to leave you? That doesn't make sense, does it?"

"I've been in a lot of relationships," she says. "It does make sense."

"How?"

"Because you'll try to push me away before I push you away."

"I don't think so."

"Why do you think I'll leave you?" Rose asks.

"I don't know. Everyone leaves eventually."

"Like your father?" she says, looking out the window. What does she see? It's only darkness and the streetlight shining on someone's car.

"No, he's different."

"Different?"

"Well, you're not my father. That's for sure."

Finally, she faces me. "Why? Just because I'm a woman? It doesn't matter. I could still feel like your father."

I look at Rose and try to see any similarity between her and my father. There is none. *You're not my father*, I think. *You're my imaginary friend.*

# TWISTER TWIRLER

Rose wants to go to the Twister Twirler fair at the park—some silly name for the annual town carnival. I haven't gone in years . . . since the summer I met a boy there who took me down to the river and made me give him a blowjob. Well, maybe not made me, but there didn't seem to be a way out of it—out of the little shack where people went fishing. He took me there, and then we started kissing, but he wanted me to do more. I said no, I didn't want to. He said, "Well, at least do this." I felt confused and decided to just do it and get it over with. There was a mattress in there, dirty as anything, but luckily he leaned against the door, and I knelt on an old quilt. I think I would be more permanently scarred if we had used the mattress, or perhaps have a disease from the experience.

We've been seeing the Twister posters around town, and Rose wants to go because it's local and she thinks it's fun. There are rides like a spider and a Ferris wheel; farm animals; contests for best cakes, pies, and pickles; greasy food and games. Rose has never been to one of these small-town fairs.

It's a warm evening when we finally get there, the day before it's closing, so the place is packed with kids and pregnant women and women with babies and teenage sweethearts wooing each other with cotton candy. Inside a building, we walk down rows and rows of cookies, cakes, and special pies awaiting judging. Rose is wearing purple shorts that make her legs look long, thin, and muscular. I'm wearing a sundress with sunflowers on it that makes me feel like I'm eight.

Rose points at some lemon pies. "I didn't know anyone still did this kind of thing," she says. "What's the fun of it?" She smiles at me mischievously.

"Baking the best pie in town. Are you serious?" I tease. "You don't see the fun in that? You can show up all your neighbors."

"Yeah, that's true. Do they ever make pot brownies? I bet those win every year."

"Kinda doubtful."

We leave the building with all of the 4-H stuff and walk around the grounds. I see a girl I know from high school holding a toddler and avoid eye contact. The little boy is holding a dirty Elmo doll and drops it on the ground. She leans over and picks it up. She notices me and smiles. I keep walking. I can't be seen. I like to imagine I am invisible. I have a feeling if I talk to someone from high school that I will become myself in high school: shy, unpopular, and not worthy of a person like Rose.

"Let's do the Ferris wheel," Rose says.

I am holding her hand, but when I see the choir director from my mom's church, I drop it. I pretend I am reaching in my bag for a mint. We wander through the crowd, and I recognize a few people here and there.

"Do you think you could ever get married and have kids?" I ask. I have a fear of sticky babies.

"Yeah, probably," she says.

"That kind of seals your fate," I say.

"What do you mean?"

"All of this." I gesture toward the kids with soggy cotton candy and the women in stretch pants and the man showing off their weight lifting muscles. "Boredom, monotony, and the American way," I say.

"I don't think so," she says.

"Why not?" I say.

"Because lesbian mothers aren't all-American, and I can be what I want."

"You think so?"

"Sure," she says and winks. "You too. We don't have to play their game."

Some days Rose seems capable of anything. I try to think about her having my baby or me having Rose's and how the baby would be both weird and invincible.

A guy is walking around selling balloon animals. "What animal do you like?" he asks Rose. She hedges because she doesn't want a balloon animal, but he makes a hippo for her anyway, saying the hippo would be a good pet for us and we could take a bath with it.

We keep walking. When we're out of earshot, I say, "Did that guy just suggest we take a bath with a balloon hippo?"

"Yeah, what kind of pervert is he?" Rose says.

We go up in the Ferris wheel. The seat is little and rickety, and I fear we will fall to our deaths, but Rose holds my hand and even puts a hand between my legs, soothing me, being bad.

We can see the river, my high school, my grandma's old house. All of it smaller and looking better from a distance, and I point all of these things out to Rose, and she asks where I went to kindergarten, and I point in the direction, and then she asks where I lost my virginity, and I point again to another spot on the small canvas before us, amazed she cares about all of these dumb places.

"Enough rides," Rose says when it's over. "Let's play some of those cheesy games. I'm good at throwing. I bet I can knock over some clowns. You know, win you something, baby." Her voice is joking, but not really joking.

A man with a big beer belly and a tattoo on his arm gives Rose the softballs. She tosses them at the clowns, all lined up. Her first throw misses. She looks very sexy as she is hurling the balls. Not throwing like a girl at all.

"Claudia."

Hearing my name, I look over the crowd. My mother is wearing a green skirt and green shoes. She looks angry and sad. She also looks kind of old. Her hair is a bit messy, with more gray streaks than I remember. I don't know the moment I started thinking about taking care of her instead of her taking care of me. I think it was around ten. That moment is back in my throat. I haven't called or seen her in months.

"Claudia," she repeats. Her face is filled with pain, and I want to take it away, but I also wish she would go away and leave me alone. Now I have to explain everything.

"I'm sorry," I say.

"Are you . . . Are you okay?"

She moves closer, and I see that she has a box of fudge under her arm.

"Yeah, I'm fine." I am forced to look at her and see how worried she's been. I sink heavily into a feeling of being a terrible daughter.

"Well, I'm not," she says. "You haven't answered my calls. You dropped off the face of the earth."

Her voice has a familiar depressed tone. I see a small opening in the crowd, and I think if I run really quickly I could speed over to the psychic's tent and hide in there.

Rose hits the clowns, and they come tumbling down, and she turns to me, her eyes wide and shining. "Hey, Claude." She laughs. "I won." Then she notices my mother.

There is no avoiding it. "This is my mother," I say. It sounds strange coming out of my mouth, as if I'm introducing someone very distant from me.

Rose smiles and says hi, then turns back to the man running the game, who is urging Rose to choose from an assortment of large animals: a huge panda, a Smurf, or a teddy bear. She points to the teddy.

My mother looks at Rose. She watches the way Rose presents me with the bear, the prize she won for me, which makes me feel funny.

"This is my friend Rose," I say.

"What's going on?" my mother says.

"Nothing," I say. "I've just been busy." I am lying and avoiding, and the guilt feels like layers of icing on a very sweet cake, so sweet it makes you ill.

"Are you seeing someone?" Her eyes dart to Rose for a second. "Fran says you're never home."

"You called Fran?" I don't know why I hadn't thought my mother would check up on me. I guess I'd just been trying not to think at all.

"You never pick up, Claudia. I was frantic."

My mother sighs and turns a sad expression on me. I am a terrible abandoner. How to explain that I'm having fun and I don't want it to end, that talking about being with Rose would be too much, when doing it is easy. How to explain that telling her would somehow make everything different.

"I've been staying with Rose," I say.

"Claudia, don't keep avoiding me. I need to see you."

My mother looks like she might cry. Part of me wants to reach for her hand, tell her I'll call, I'll come over tomorrow, but something stops me. I know it isn't true.

My mother walks away, and the man who runs the throwing booth, who looks like he just got out of jail and has a tattoo on his arm of a very thin woman with large breasts, shakes his head at me and says, "Be nice to your mom, sweetie."

I want to snap, "What do you know about it?" but as I open my mouth, I see he looks haggard, like he probably does know something about almost everything. "I will," I say to him.

"My mother's gone," he says. "She was a saint, and I was her sinner. It's my nature." He laughs. "But maybe I could have tried a little harder." Then, turning from us, he raises his voice: "Three balls for a dollar. Knock 'em down. Win the big bear like this little lady right here. Just had a big winner. Three balls for a dollar."

"So that's your Mom," Rose says.

"Yeah," I say. "I'm sorry if she was rude."

"No," Rose says. "I think I liked her."

I look to see if she's being sarcastic, but her face is truthful.

"You could tell she really loves you," Rose says in a low voice, almost whispering, and I think I hear a hint of envy.

# OLD GIRLFRIEND

Rose's old girlfriend is in town, and I can't breathe. Rose picked her up at the train station, took her out to dinner somewhere, and then probably for drinks and God knows what else. Robin is visiting for the weekend to get away from a bad situation in Philly. All of Rose's exes seem troubled: abusive fathers, no money, on the verge of homelessness, drug addicts. Robin has been through rehab and is now trying to avoid her friends who use drugs. She wants to get away from the city, get some fresh air. I freaked out when Rose told me she was coming, and Rose said I can't be so jealous, that she has lots of friends and most of her exes are her friends and she can't be babying me. I agreed to let her and Robin have this night together to reconnect and talk, and then we would get together in the morning.

It's 2:30 a.m. I am obsessing. I lie in bed thinking about what great sex Rose and her ex are having, how they are probably entering different astral realms or doing it on every possible surface of the house or, like the porn movie, with carrots, or anal sex, or maybe they are out and attacking each other in the bathroom at Brett's bar, shoving themselves against the door so nobody can come in.

I must stop myself. There are places the mind doesn't need to go. I can't sleep and I can't call her and I need to know what's going on. Who is sleeping where and are they having sex right now? I can't call; the phone is an enemy of love, and I should trust Rose.

I hear the neighbor's dog barking again and want to report them to the police. They have this black dog that they keep on a short rope, and they shut him out so he barks at night and drives everyone nuts, but nobody says anything because the people who own him are kind of redneck and throw beer cans out their windows and have Fourth of July parties where they basically light off the whole street. I hear a siren. Like the man in "The Tell-Tale Heart," I feel like my every sense is magnified. I think I hear Fran's cats moving around, trees swaying in the wind, a car alarm a mile away, birds flying by, Rose and Robin moaning.

I get out of bed and pull a shirt and sweatpants over my pajamas. I walk to Rose's house. I could drive, but I need to think. At this hour, there aren't many cars around. Maybe I should be scared, but I'm not. People don't get killed very often in Riverton. When they do, it's by their husbands or lovers. Some guys ride by in a pick-up truck and look at me hard, but they don't stop or even yell. It's a thick August night, with mosquitoes and the smell of rotting things and flowers in the air. The grass is lush and green, the way it gets in late summer, just becoming more and more of a jungle until the fall hits. I feel a bit of the wild in me. I look terrible. I've been crying on and off over the night and drinking wine, which I shouldn't have done. I feel all weepy, and I want Rose to hold me, but I'm afraid she'll be angry.

Her door looks scary and totally different. I notice for the first time a sticker on it about a security dog, left over from whoever owned the house before. The door is wood, and there is a knocker that I never use as well as a doorbell. I also have a key, but using that would seem like invasion, and what if they really are having sex and I go in there? I can't ring the bell because I'm afraid of waking the ex-girlfriend and looking desperate and her wondering what's wrong with me. I pick up a little rock and throw it at Rose's bedroom window. Maybe she'll hear and let me in. Maybe she'll be happy to see me. I throw more rocks at her window, just little rocks. Nothing is happening. A neighbor is just coming home and eyes me with suspicion as they click their garage door opener and let themselves in.

Nothing happens. Maybe she doesn't hear. I throw a bigger rock. It makes a loud sound. I'm afraid it might break the window, but it doesn't. After another rock, the light goes on in the bedroom. Then the living room light goes on, and then the porch light. Then the door opens, and I see the silhouette. Rose comes outside alone.

"Claudia, Jesus, you scared me. I almost called the police. What's wrong? What are you doing here?"

She is wearing a robe and underneath it her old man pajamas with pinstripes. She sounds angry.

"I'm sorry," I say. "I couldn't sleep."

"Baby, you shouldn't have come at this hour. It's not good."

"I just kept thinking about you."

"You don't trust me, do you?" She folds her hands in front of her chest.

"Yes, I do." I say, but it sounds false. "Where's your friend?" I look past her, but it's all darkness. What do I expect—a naked woman?

"She's sleeping. It's three o'clock in the morning. She's going to think you're psycho."

"Can I come in? Just let me sleep here." I am standing mere feet from her. I reach for her hand, but she backs away.

"Okay, but don't touch me. I don't like these games."

I follow her into the house.

"You look terrible," she says.

I know that I look terrible, but I don't want her to say it. "I couldn't sleep. I was worried about you."

"Shhh," she says. "I don't want to have to explain this to Robin. You weren't worried about me. You were worried I would do something," she whispers.

"I'm sorry," I say. I regret coming here. I regret my thoughts. I regret breathing.

"Don't be sorry," she says. "Just don't try to control everything."

We get into bed, and she turns off the light. It feels like there is a great distance between us.

She whispers, "It's hard enough getting used to living here without feeling controlled."

"I thought that you loved it here," I say.

"I do, in a way, but I have no friends, no other lesbians. We're too isolated. I can't drop my whole life for you."

"Do you want to leave me?" *It's happening*, I think. *She's breaking up with me.*

"No, Claudia, just relax a little."

If only she could see how impossible this request is. "I didn't know you were so unhappy," I say. "I thought you were happy."

"I am, baby. It's not so black and white."

We sleep without having sex, on opposite sides of the bed. I don't even rest my hand on her stomach.

# THE TRUTH

"Why don't we play a game where we tell each other our worst truths?"
I say to Rose.

She is on the other side of the checkout desk at the library. She looks
at me with suspicion.

I came to see her in the library like I used to in the early days, when
I first fell for her. I spied on her for a bit first. I went to the far table
and sat next to a girl who was writing a report on Vincent van Gogh.
Over her shoulder I saw the pictures of his art and thought about what
it would be like to be so in love with color that you'd go hungry for it. I
watched Rose checking out books with an air of calm focus. I watched
her for fifteen minutes before she noticed.

Ever since Robin came to town, things haven't been the same between Rose and me. Lately, Rose scares me. I feel like I've been looking
for a lover forever, and now, when she is here, I can't cut it. When Rose
looks me in the eyes, I'm afraid I'm going to suffocate.

"That sounds macabre," she says now. "What's the point? Isn't it kind
of juvenile?"

"Well, yeah, I guess I'm juvenile. And macabre and dramatic."

"I didn't say dramatic."

"You should have."

I woke up this morning knowing I need to tell Rose my darkest secret.
There is a lie that I've been holding onto, and it's festering inside of me, or
to be more truthful it keeps me from feeling close to her. It makes me cold.

"It's okay to have strong emotions. I'm not going to tell you to turn
them off."

She smiles. She likes me. I can see that. She goes for things I want to do even if she thinks they're wrong. She caves in the way I've always seen women cave to things men want because they're their men. It makes me feel guilty.

She looks so beautiful with her long hair, wearing a nice blue shirt and brown slacks. She always looks well put together for work. I like to think of her here. It soothes me to think of her putting her hands on all of the books. Sometimes I imagine I'm a book, and she's putting her hands on my spine.

Rose told me how she had fallen in love with books in the rare book room at the Philadelphia library. She volunteered at the library and became friends with someone in the rare book room. They would let her handle early Shakespeare manuscripts and medieval texts. Each book was like a message from another person, she said. An attempt at communication. I think she would love me more if I were a rare book.

"Why do we need to do this?" she asks. "Is there really some big secret?"

"I don't know," I say. "I just need to."

I don't want to tell her she doesn't know things about me—awful things I've done—and once she knows she might not like me anymore.

"Okay," she says. "I'll do it."

That night I go over to her place, and we make pasta with gravy together, or rather I start to help, but there isn't that much to do, so I just enjoy watching Rose cook. She learned Italian cooking from her nana and has an exact way of doing things with a sharp knife, dicing the garlic so elegantly. We don't talk about the game until after dinner. There is a thunderstorm coming. I have felt it in the air all day, and now it's raining hard and we hear the far-off thunder.

We sit on her sofa together. In the place most people would have a television, she has a card catalog she got from the library where she worked in Philadelphia. They were throwing them away, so she decided to take one and then made a mini card catalog of her own books. I see a flash of lightning in the window.

"So," Rose says. "Who goes first?" She is wearing a green shirt and green pants, and she looks like an elf, a beautiful elf, an elf leader princess.

"Why don't you?" I say.

"That's nice. Your game. I go first." Rose has an expression of disinterest, of doing this because she has to. "Okay, I'm just supposed to tell you bad things. No truth or dare? Only truth. Right?"

"Yes, we can go back and forth in rounds, and what we say should keep getting worse."

"Okay," she says. "When I was little I picked on another girl in school and told her she'd been wearing the same outfit the day before."

"It's hard to picture you doing that," I say.

"Really?" she says. "But kids are cruel."

"Yeah, but you seem like you would be such a nice kid."

There is a boom of thunder so loud it makes me jump. The rain is coming down hard. In our early days together we would have gone out on the porch to sit and watch the storm, content in our own bubble, but now it's all different.

"Anyway, that's nothing," Rose says.

I sense she has now become competitive, wanting to win the game. To admit the bigger badness.

I say, "Well, I broke Hal's heart by going out with you. I never told you, but we were sort of seeing each other before you came along."

"I know that," Rose says. "I'm not blind, and besides, Hal and I talked about it. He seems okay. I don't get how you could be into someone so old, but I think it makes you interesting."

"But I really hurt him."

Her expression hasn't changed. She is not happy with this game, and I am not impressing her. "That's what people do in relationships," she says.

I see a glimmer of the possibility of her turning on me and walking away. I picture myself talking to Rose in the future, and her just staring coolly at me. All that we have together now will be a dream then—or not a dream, but a nightmare, because it will have meant nothing to her.

"I think you can do worse," she says, and I suddenly fear what she'll say next. I am creating evil in this relationship.

"I had a sort of boyfriend one time," she says, "but I didn't really like him, so when we were supposed to go on a date, I told him I would meet him at the movie theater, but I never showed up."

"Ouch!" I laugh a little, relieved.

"Yeah, I could be cruel."

There is another flash of lightning. She turns to look out the window. The pine trees are shaking in the wind, and water is pooling in the ditch in her backyard.

"Okay," I say. "Well, once I punched a boy in the face for throwing a ball at me in gym. I didn't like to be hit."

"How old were you?" she asks.

"Thirteen."

"I guess that's bad, but who can control anything they do at thirteen? We're all hormone bags," she says. "I thought you wanted really bad things. Here's something. I got so pissed off at my old girlfriend that I put her things on the street, and it was like a giant party, all these people stopping and taking stuff. Kind of a yard sale but no prices, and when she found out, she punched me in the stomach."

"Jesus," I say. "She hit you? For real?"

"Yeah, it was fucked up." The color has drained from Rose's face.

"Why did you put her stuff on the street?"

"She was sleeping with my friend. Cute little Kimmy. Fuck her. Is that bad enough for you? I mean, I can get worse. Not that I think this is a good idea, Claude."

The game is horrible, and she is winning.

"That sounds really rough."

"It was the worst breakup ever, like raining shit. What about you?"

*What about me? What about me?*

"I think I killed my father."

It's out of my mouth in a second and can't be taken back. My revelation is underscored by another boom of thunder.

"What are you talking about? You would know if you killed someone."

Rose is looking at me with what seems to be pity, as if I'm the most desperate person she could imagine.

"He disappeared. I don't really know if he left us. The night he went missing, I was thinking about poisoning him."

"You're fucking with me." She gets up and walks to the window. "Is this another one of your fantasy tales?"

The thunder is inside me now. The storm is making my crazy. "No. The night he disappeared, I had a dream about poisoning him, and in the morning, there was rat poison on the kitchen table. All I know is I was very angry, and in the middle of the night I thought about getting up and putting rat poison in his orange juice."

Rose's back is to me, and she's looking at the mess outside. The pine trees' branches move like a drunk trying to regain balance.

I get up and stand beside her. "Maybe I did that. I'm not sure. I had so many nightmares on top of each other. I dreamed I had poisoned him, and I dreamed I went out to check if the poison was on the shelf in the basement. Then it was on the kitchen counter, and I don't know how it got there."

"Wait," she says. "I thought your father just left your mother, abandoned you."

"It's not that simple. I found out my father was cheating on my mother, and I confronted him about it. The next day he was gone, and I never said anything to anyone about the poison. I never talked to my mother about it."

Rose turns from the window and looks at me intensely. "Dreaming isn't doing. This is not true," she says. "You would know if you killed someone. But why do you think you killed him?"

"I wanted to so much, and I really don't know what happened."

"Doesn't it make more sense that he just left?"

"But what about the poison on the counter?"

"If he was poisoned, wouldn't there be a body?"

"Yeah, I've thought about that. Either my mother buried it because she saw the poison and knew what I'd done, or maybe he went for a walk to think about things and died out there somewhere."

Rose looks skeptical. "Doesn't it seem a little odd to you that nobody ever found the body? In mysteries, if there's no body, there's no crime. You seriously think your mother buried the body of your father and never told you? What is this, a made-for-TV movie?"

Rose doesn't understand. She thinks I'm crazy. Maybe I am. Hearing her be so logical makes me doubt myself, but even as I wonder, I can't stop talking. In a strange way, it feels good to speak, to let my secret out.

"When I see that night," I say, "I remember I had this urge to go to the basement. When I turned on the light, I saw the rat poison on the shelf. It had a picture of a rat with an X over its body and the word POISON on it. I had this awful thought—that I could punish my father. Make him sick. I wanted to hurt him the way he'd hurt me. The way he was hurting my mom. I don't remember what happened next, but when I woke up, I found the rat poison in the kitchen."

Once again Rose's expression has changed. Now I think I see compassion in her eyes.

"Do you really think you killed your father?" she asks. "Like truly, deep down, or is this a fear that some part of you knows isn't real?"

"I can't tell," I say. "That's the scary part. When I told you the story just now, it seemed implausible, but I think there's still a possibility. There is a doubt, and I'll never be sure."

Rose is staring off into the distance with the look of someone making a plan. "What if you found him?"

Of course, I have thought of this, thought of doing searches or traveling to look, picking up a phone books to see if he is listed, but something always stopped me.

"Maybe," I say.

"Maybe."

Her voice is clear and brisk, like a therapist's. I think, *My God, she's my therapist.* I'm the worst lover ever. I look at her there, in her green outfit. Green, the color of hope, yet I am hopeless. I have always been.

"So you are saying if you found your father alive then maybe you would believe that you hadn't poisoned him," she says.

"Well, if I knew it was really him and not somebody with the same name, then I'd know he hadn't died. Maybe I still poisoned him, but I didn't kill him. I realize I sound crazy, but this is what I feel."

"Well, that would be a place to start, wouldn't it? Concrete proof."

I've been trying so long to get my mind around that night, thinking if I could go back in time and remember better, I'd know what happened, but Rose is trying to pull me forward. Finding my father is another way of learning the truth, but the idea has always seemed like a defeat. If he is alive, then why the hell doesn't he find me? I'm his daughter, and I don't need to go begging to some wizened old cheater like him. This is what I'm thinking, but I know if I say it, Rose will find a way with her superior logic to turn the tables.

"You're right," I say, not sure what I mean.

"So what if we tried to find him?"

She looks so concerned that it frightens me. I feel like I am making her care for me, but I don't want her help.

"Hey, wait," I say. "Rose—I don't want you looking for my father. It's creepy to think about."

Just the thought of him seeing her sickens me, as if she lives in one world and he lives in another, and if the two worlds meet, everything will become shitty.

"Well, if we found him, you could stop thinking you killed him."

"But what if we never find him? Then I'd know he was dead for sure, and I killed him."

"Or he moved to another country. Or died from some other cause."

I can't help but think that she would enjoy the whole business— doing the research, eliminating possibilities, tracking him down. She's making me feel like the last ten years of my life have been a joke. Like I could have just done this simple thing and avoided all my crazy guilt.

"Just forget it," I say. "I don't want to dredge this up. If I find him, I'd have to tell Mom, and then she'd feel awful all over again. You've convinced me. I didn't kill him. He's alive somewhere, just nowhere I want to know about."

Rose sees right through me. She crosses her arms. "Come on. You just don't want me to look. What's his name, anyway?"

"I don't remember," I say. My skin is on fire.

"What is his name?"

"It's not important." My stomach is an open sore.

"Just tell me. It's the first step to finding him."

"Listen, Rose." My voice is rising; I am almost yelling. "I don't want you to look for him."

"Then why the hell did you tell me the story?" She's raised her voice too.

"I thought I could trust you."

"You want to find him," she says with a stubborn set to her jaw.

"You think you know what I want all of the time. You think you understand me, but you don't."

I pick up my keys from the table and head to the door.

"Oh, right. Leave. You set up this whole fucking game so you can tell me your secret, and now you don't want to do anything about it?"

"I told you. I thought that was enough."

Now I'm crying, and she is crying too, and I can't stand any of it. I just need to get out of here. Rose can't solve this problem for me.

"I need to go," I say. "I'm sorry. I can't breathe."

"Stay," Rose says urgently. "We'll talk about it in the morning. No more talk now."

"I can't," I say. "I feel like I'm suffocating and if I stay here one more minute I'll black out."

Rose is shaking her head back and forth, saying no with her body. "Claudia, I can't take this. If you go, then don't come back. I moved here to get away from all the drama. Do you understand? Do you understand that I feel things too, and I can't have my emotions pulled around like this?"

"Yes," I say. "I don't want drama either. I don't want anything."

She opens the door, pushes me through, and closes it behind me. I run through the rain to my car. There is flash of lightning close by, and I scream. I struggle getting my key in the lock, then the door opens. Inside it is dry and mine. My car. My space.

I look down. On the seat next to me is a note Rose wrote me a few days ago and left on my dashboard: *Chase me. I'll let you catch me.*

Notes are like little knives. They always hold the feeling after the feeling is over.

# THAT NIGHT

I'm not able to sleep. I still have childish sheets on my bed. They have Cinderella on them, even though I don't like her. My mom got them at a yard sale. "They're in perfect shape," she said, and even though I wanted purple sheets, or ones with daisies on them, I put that out of my mind and took the Cinderella ones.

After my confrontation with my father, I didn't sleep, either. I just lay in my bed and waited until I heard him go out. I drifted off then, but woke later to the sound of my parents arguing. The orange numbers of my digital clock read 2:19.

I can hear what happens in the living room clearly.

"Jesus, what did you expect?" It's my father's voice. Slurring a little. "You keep nagging after me, and what do you really expect?"

"I'm sorry," my mother says in the voice of the grass.

"What did you fucking expect?"

"I'm sorry," she says in the voice of the dirt.

"Well, I can't eat this. I can't eat it now. It's cold."

"I'm sorry," she says in the voice of the tangled, the voice of the small, the voice of the fearful.

"You're always sorry," he says.

"Okay," she says. "I'm not sorry. Is that better? I'm not fucking sorry!" she yells. "You were out until all hours, and I couldn't keep it warm. How could I?"

*Wow,* I think. *Mom is fighting back.*

And then I hear it, the sound of his hand hitting her. The sound of her sucking in her breath, the sound of her cry, and then quiet.

"I'm sorry," she says. In the voice of the dead.

I lie there for a long time. I try to not think. If I go out there, they will both yell at me. My mother has told me to never, ever interfere when they are fighting. I know she is afraid for me. Sometimes my father has been just on the edge of hitting me. I could see it in his eyes. But each time he pulled back.

One time I came out and yelled at my father to stop, and he yelled at me to stay out of his fucking business, and my mother pushed me back into my room. She threatened me: *If you come out here, I will spank you.* He took his anger out on her afterward. I cried myself to sleep.

Now I don't sleep. I wait. I wait until they are finally quiet. I wait, and I plan, with hatred in my heart. She will have a bruise on her face tomorrow. She will put on the layers of foundation and powder. She will be too ashamed to go out. She will lie about what happened. She will be a liar. He will be a liar. She will be his liar.

If I killed him, would we be happier? If I killed him, he wouldn't hurt my mother. He wouldn't be a threat to me. But I might go to jail, and then I could be raped or beaten with a club. Also, I don't want to hurt my mother. She might still love him. He can be nice sometimes.

I get up quietly. They are somehow asleep now. Sleeping off the anger, the hitting. Sleeping because it's better than thinking. I find myself in the basement. I don't remember deciding to come here. The stairs are steep, and the walls are unfinished stone. The only things down here are laundry and cleaning products. I am staring up at the shelf, at a brown bottle that says Rat and Mouse Poison. Last year we had a rat in the basement, and my mother found some old poison and got rid of it. The shelf is high, but not too high. I stand on my tiptoes and just reach the bottle. I jiggle it forward, and then it's in my hand, and I take it down without breaking it. I hold it in my fist like anger. I walk upstairs.

Inside, my stomach is rolling a ball of sickness. I want it to roll into his stomach, to transfer this illness to its source. I want to make a meal of my pain and feed it to him. I could go to his bed when he is sleeping and hit him over and over. I could take a bat, but then he might wake up and use it on me, kill me. I don't want to die. I just want everything to change. I think about when I gave him Mike's note—the look of contempt on his face, the fact that he thinks Mom deserves no respect, that I deserve no respect. I want to punish him. To make him hurt.

I stand in the kitchen. I don't think. This is not an intention. It's an action. Something I just *do*. I remember the orange juice. My father always drinks it in the morning. Mom doesn't. She says it's too sweet for her.

I turn the brown bottle in my hand. On the label it says to use one teaspoon and mix it in with some food or sweet water. I use my mom's measuring spoons, like I would for a recipe for chocolate chip cookies. Then I get out the orange juice, which mom makes from tubes of frozen concentrate and then stores in a pitcher in the fridge.

I stir in one teaspoon of rat poison and put the pitcher back, promising myself I'll throw out the rest after my father has some in the morning. I wash the spoon. I dry it. I put it away. I go to bed. Somehow, Claudia-the-poisoner can sleep.

Later, I will tell myself that I didn't want to kill him. That he's much bigger than a rat. I only wanted to make him sick. Give him pain. Still later I will forget whether it really happened at all.

# MATCH GIRL

I have ruined my life. It's been three days since I left Rose's house. To-night I had a fantasy about the little match girl. Not a sexual fantasy; that would be sick. The little match girl is poor and homeless and without her grandmother. In the fantasy, I am homeless and sleeping outside of Rose's door. She comes home and sees me there. It's been years since she's seen me, and I have wasted away into what I now feel like—a being with no soul and eyes of blackest black. I am trying to light a fire with a poem that I wrote for her. "Look at this," I say. "I wrote you this poem." She walks past me with her girlfriend, who smells like a sexy perfume and is wearing a cute 1950s dress that is way too short for anyone who doesn't have legs like she does. They disappear into the pink bungalow. I think that maybe if I put the poem under the door, Rose will find it.

I drank too much last night and had other terrible fantasies, the kind that burrow into your skin, into your head like an earwig. Do earwigs really burrow into your brain? Or is that another fantasy? I picked up the phone to ask Rose but didn't call. I couldn't dial the last digit.

What Rose doesn't understand is I can't be brave like her. I can't find my father, and I can't eat beef, and I can't do anything. I can't tell her the whole truth about what happened, how I poisoned him. Something like that makes me irredeemable, even in my own eyes. How could anyone ever trust me after that?

# SELF-PUNISHMENT

Today I tried to call Rose several times, but she didn't answer. I wonder if she is avoiding me and, if so, how long it will last. At work I did a study of all of the objects in the food vending machine for nutritional value, which amounts to almost nothing, since most are made of pure sugar. The pretzels (the women's mags say) are lowest in fat and calories, and peanut butter crackers have some protein, which is the kind of information I've stored in my brain for no reason, the kind of information that we have these days and carry with us like the extra weight of a tumor. I have no food in my house to pack a lunch and no desire to go out, so I have been eating my way through the machine. It's a small form of self-punishment. I had a microwave burrito today and Junior Mints, which are nowhere on anyone's list of healthy food.

Junior Mints remind me of the movies, with their waxy surface and the smell on my hands after I eat them. As I finished the box, I had the feeling of being a kid and sneaking into extra movies at the mall, holding the mints in my hands.

I call Rose, and the phone rings and rings, the answering machine picks up, and I try to sense if she is in the room, listening to my message. I can't tell. I don't have a sixth sense, though one part of me thinks she is there and hating me, and another part of me thinks she is at the movies the way I was as a kid, avoiding going home, forgetting everything.

# SPECIAL ROOM

Luke is at his desk, pushing paperclips into a pile. He has moved up a bit in the hierarchy, getting hired on full time to do work just a little above temp work. He has access to the supply closet now. I walk up to him, and he sees in my face that something horrible has happened.

Life is bad. I have fucked up. I do wrong things over and over. Now the toxins in the atmosphere are eating on my brain cells, and I will never jump a boxcar, and I will never again hold anything as sweet as Rose in my mouth, and here I am in hell again.

My gut feels rotten, like I drank coffee and whiskey on an empty stomach and maybe topped it off with some turpentine. I almost got high on cough syrup last night. I took some to try to sleep and couldn't sleep and drank some more and then, in the middle of the night, my mouth rimmed with cherry mucus thickness, drank even more and felt floaty. My head hurts, and my insides. I look at Luke through a haze of pain.

His eyes widen. "What's wrong with you, Claudia?" he asks.

"I don't know," I say, knowing, knowing, but unable to form it into a sentence.

"You want to go somewhere and talk?"

I nod, and he takes my hand and leads me down the hallway. I don't notice what other people are doing or whether they think this is inappropriate. Everything is inappropriate. Everything is wrong.

Luke leads me to his special place. He has found a room that's being used to store old office equipment, where nobody ever goes. It's beyond the door to the fire escape, up a short staircase. He has a small library of books in there and regularly retreats to the room for philosophical pondering and reading. On some shelves are a bunch of technical manuals from the '50s and some old typewriters. Luke has set up a desk with one of the typewriters and has a few of his books in a row on the corner of it, along with a can with some flowers.

"What's wrong?" he asks. "Is it Rose?"

"I don't even know what happened," I say.

"Did she break up with you?"

"I think I broke up with her, but I wanted her back immediately and then it was too late. Or maybe I just can't deal with her. I don't know." I am crying.

"You need a drink," Luke says and opens the drawer of the old wooden desk. In the bottom, under a 1972 phonebook, he has a pint of Jack Daniels. He hands me the bottle, and I take a swig. It's like fire, numbing all sensation in my mouth; I can see why people drink.

"I'm so stupid," I say.

"No, you're not. I did that once. The first guy I ever slept with. I just ran away from his house in the middle of the night. The next day I wanted to see him. I kept calling him, and he never called back. Of course, he lived with his parents, so I couldn't exactly beg them to let me talk to their son, my lover."

"She's shut me out. I was stupid and scared, and now she won't have anything to do with me."

"It's okay," he says, looking at me seriously. "You're not as old as you think you are, Claudia. It's okay to not know what you want. It's okay to fuck up."

"But what if she was the one?"

"Listen," Luke says. "You need to leave this town. I'm moving to San Francisco. I have a friend there. Why don't you come with me?"

The idea stuns me, pulling me out of the mire of self-pity. Leaving Riverton. Something I've dreamed of forever but thought would never happen. Leaving my past behind. Living a life somewhere else.

"It's cool, right?" I say, tentative. "Gays and hippies?"

"Yeah, something like that. I think the hippies are gone, but it's a hell of a lot more exciting than this place." He smiles.

Could I move there with him? I can't believe I'm considering it. "When are you leaving?" I ask.

"In a month." He puts his feet up on the desk.

"I don't know if I can," I say. But maybe I could. I feel like all of the air has been sucked out of me. San Francisco could fill me back up.

"Well, now seems like a good time," he says. "My friend thinks he can get me a job. Maybe he can help you too. Without Rose, what's here for you?"

"Nothing," I say and start crying again.

"A new place will clear you mind." He pats the top of my head. "There'll be a lot more women like Rose there. A lot more people like us."

How hard this town must be for him, how claustrophobic with his parents and the church looking at him all the time. When they speak in tongues, what do they say about their son? He told me they believe AIDS is sent from God to wipe out homosexuals.

I think about my walks around the town. I think about the library and Hal and my mother and the river and how much I hate this place . . . and how much underneath it all I love this place. It's like a sickness in me. I do hate it, and I do love it. They are both true, but the biggest truth is that I hate myself for staying here, for feeling stuck, for complaining. If I stay, I think I'll just hate myself more and more.

# BLUE

I wake up in the middle of the night with nobody next to me. I think of Rose's sweet breasts and the warmth between her legs and how she would sometimes kiss me all over, starting at the tip of my head, working her way down, and then biting my feet. The pain comes in waves. It's 2:00 a.m. I've just tried to call Rose, and of course she didn't answer. I need to see her now. I think about going to her house and knocking on the door, but she won't answer. I call my mother.

"Mom," I say, choking back the tears.

"Honey, my God. Claudia, it's two o'clock. Are you okay?"

Her voice sounds sleepy and worried. I feel bad for calling her like this, for making her think something terrible has happened, but something terrible has happened.

"Mom, it's Rose." I say. I don't want to explain, but I need to tell her. I need to confess everything. "We broke up," I say. "We weren't just friends. I was in love with her." My words rasp out, as if someone is strangling me. I'm afraid my mother will turn on me too, think I'm a stranger. That she won't want to be the mother of a lesbian.

"I thought maybe," my mother says. "Are you okay? Do you want to come over?"

I want to. I want to go to my mother's house. I want to be held. It's juvenile. It's awful. I trudge to the car. I'm in my nightgown. It's starting to rain. There is a thundershower. The sky is so beautiful, flashes of lightning showing off the lushness everywhere. I want to throw up. Why is anything beautiful? I start driving, but as I pass Rose's house, I turn around and stop. I get out and walk to the door. I am dripping wet, standing in front of what used to seem like my home. I am not welcome here. If I knocked, she wouldn't let me in. There is a clap of thunder. I startle and run back to the car, soaking my seat, and drive to my mother's house.

Mom opens the door and gives me a hug even though I'm very wet. Pulling me inside, she tells me to take off my clothes. I'm embarrassed that she is seeing me naked, so I keep my underwear on.

"Take them off," she says. "I have some of your things around here." She leaves me in the foyer briefly, then returns with a towel, a flannel nightgown, and an old pair of my underwear with flowers on them. They are not roses.

While I dress, she makes hot chocolate, then we sit in the living room and drink it. I am crying, and she is letting me, being so nice it makes me feel guilty for ignoring her all of these months, even though I want her to be nice to me. I need it so badly.

"It's okay, baby," she says. "Everyone gets their heart broke sometime. I'm sorry."

Does she mean Dad? Something was broken when he disappeared. Maybe all of me. Maybe that's why I am like this. Unlovable.

"I know it's cliché, but it will get better with time. You won't always feel this way."

Is that how it was with my father? I know she was sad, but also re-lieved, when he was gone. She wasn't the one expecting the police to come to the door. She wasn't waiting for the crime lab to find traces of rat poison in his body. *Body*. Where was his body?

"Why did Dad leave us?" I have nothing to lose. I'm alone, and I've fucked up my life, and I might as well know the truth.

She looks surprised for a second, then answers, "He didn't want to be married, and he didn't want to stop drinking. He wanted to do what he wanted."

Something feels stuck in my throat. I swallow. "He's not dead, is he?"

When I say this, her eyes flash on me for a second with pain and a kind of shock.

"No, he's not dead. Did you think he was?" She reaches out and puts her hand on my arm.

"I didn't know. Are you sure?" What if she's lying to me, protecting me?

"Yes," she says calmly, taking a sip of the chocolate. "He sent me legal documents. For the divorce."

She got a divorce? They exchanged legal papers? "I didn't know that either," I say. "Why didn't you ever talk about it?" Why did she hide everything from me, like I had nothing to do with my father at all?

"I guess I just wanted to forget about him," she says. "I thought he would take some time away and then come back and want to see you. But he never did, and I wasn't sure what to say." She meets my eyes. "I was so afraid of him," she says, "but I was more afraid of how you looked at me when I was with him. You looked sorry for me, and I couldn't take that."

I shut my eyes. *I'm not a murderer.* I take a breath and release it, feeling tears trickle down my face. I'm not a murderer, just unwanted. I kept waiting years and years for him to come back. I hear the storm beyond the window, and I think about going out there and lying on the ground. Maybe if I did I would be struck by lightning, right in the heart, and die instantly. "He never tried to contact me."

"I'm sorry, honey. You can probably track him down if you want. I have an address from a few years ago, in Texas."

Through my tears, she looks like a giant flower sitting there across from me.

"But I think he's drinking a lot," she continues. "He's probably not much to look at."

"Doesn't it seem at all strange to you that my father just disappeared one day and we never talked about it?" I say, my voice cracking.

"I know," she says. "It's wrong. The first winter all I could do was cry, and then after that, when it started to hurt less, I wanted to forget. He was so mean sometimes. I thought we were better not thinking about him, moving on. Did you miss him?"

"Did I miss him?" My sadness morphs. I feel suddenly angry, very angry. I think about slapping her—how it would feel good for a minute, but then I would just be sad. Of course I think of slapping her; that's what he taught me. "Yes, Mom. What do you think? He was my father. I mean, I hated him, but I missed him."

"He wasn't very good to us."

I can hear the pain in her voice and I remember hearing him hit her, how afterward she looked like a frightened animal.

"No, he wasn't. I missed him even before he was gone. Sometimes he could be very sweet, but I never knew when those times would be, and I wanted them to last."

"I know," she says. "He could be sweet sometimes."

She is hunches over, drawing herself in so she looks smaller than she is, but she is not as little as she was the day she said sorry a million times. She will never be that little again.

I swipe the moisture from my cheeks. "I thought that I would be with Rose forever," I say.

My mother scoots closer and wraps an arm around my shoulder. "I'm so sorry. I know it hurts, but you'll be okay."

Will I? I don't know if that's true. I think of the orange juice, the poison. How I lied to Rose.

"What if I've done something terribly wrong? Won't it hurt more each day, until I die?"

She shakes her head. "No, baby, even if you've done something terribly wrong, it will still hurt less and less."

What is it about time that makes us so uncaring and numb? Everyone talks about it like it's a really good drug.

I sleep in the same bed with my mother, like I sometimes did after Dad left. She holds me next to her and strokes my hair. She's wearing an old cotton nightgown, and when I put my head on her chest, she smells a little like Bengay. In the night she snores slightly and tosses in her sleep.

*game eleven*

# SURVIVAL

I don't want to play any sex games anymore. Now I want to play life and death games. We are in the Arctic together. The dog has died, and now we are pulling the sled ourselves. We're so fucking hungry. We eat the dog. We eat some left-over seal fat. I feel the frost get into my toes and know I will definitely lose a few. They are turning black like rotted mushrooms. We must work hard to keep each other warm. What happened before and what might happen later don't mean anything. Your love and heat are all that matter to me in this moment. It's thirty below zero, and if our skin is exposed for mere seconds, it starts to freeze. You make me warm coverings for my feet. I sew you into your clothes when you go out hunting. We pull the goddamn sled. Surviving together is a game we play and play over again. I make you squeeze the fat into my mouth. I am looking into your deep eyes, and I see many lifetimes reflected there. You scrape the last meat off of the rabbit and give it to me. We are tired all day. You say, "If I die, eat me," and I say, "What if we're starving, little by little, right now?" We boil the bones and eat them.

# MY MOTHER DYING

When I get in my car and head to San Francisco, I picture my mother dying. I have decided to follow Luke, who has a room in his place for me. Some apartment with five people in a sketchy part of town—a little dangerous, but fun, he says. Really fun. His roommates include a massage therapist, an activist, a graphic designer, and a writer who works at a café.

Telling my coworkers I was leaving was one of the most exhilarating experiences of my life. They all seemed shocked and concerned that I didn't have another job. I have $890 saved and another paycheck coming. I'll survive.

As I take the highway out of town, I have fantasies of my mother on her deathbed, alone. I am leaving everything sweet we had together. Abandoning her. I am the prodigal daughter. I am denying her. Last night she called and asked if I was really going away, and I said, "I guess so." Am I scared? Yes. Packing was horrible, and I cried as I loaded everything into boxes, especially when I found things of Rose's, but I have to go.

"Who will visit me?" she asked.

"I'll visit you at the holidays and call you every week," I promised.

"It's lonely getting old," she said.

"You're not old, Mom. Maybe you should try dating."

"Okay, Claudia, go," she said, and the phone clicked.

Did she hang up on me? I didn't call her back and she didn't call me back; I guess that's hanging up.

Now I smell like sweat and pussy juice and like the smashed-up grass and dirt. After the conversation with my mother, I fell asleep, but then woke up in the middle of the night feeling manic, with a very clear idea of absolute certainty: I must see Rose.

I got up and put my jeans on. I drove over to her house. I started throwing rocks at her window like that insane night when Robin was there. After a few stones, she came out into the yard, yelling, "Jesus, you scared me. What the fuck are you doing?"

"I'm leaving town," I said.

"Really," she said, crossing her arms over her chest. "I thought you were never going to leave."

I searched for some softness in her look, but her face was dark. She had closed a door to me and she was not opening it.

"I'm sorry that I blew things with us," I said. "I know it was my fault. Luke moved to San Francisco, and he told me to come live with him for a while and find a job. I'm heading out tomorrow."

"Good," she said. "You need to leave this town."

There was something about the way she phrased this. Not *I want you to leave*, but *You need to leave*. Like despite herself she was considering me—what was best for me. "I cried for weeks thinking of you," I said.

She kicked the ground with her slipper. "If you're leaving, what are you doing here?" she asked.

"I guess I want you to forgive me," I said. "And to tell you I've missed you. And I wanted to say goodbye."

She shook her head as if I were a dim child and she was so much wiser. Then she shocked me by stepping forward and putting her arms around me. "Goodbye," she said.

We stood there for a long time, hugging. Then she pulled me even closer, and I felt the warmth of her. I touched her hair and pressed against her body, so familiar to me. She started kissing me, and then I was kissing her, burning up with all I felt. I pulled her to the ground and started having sex with her in the yard—a mad confusion blending the thoughts *I have to leave* and *I have to touch her*. She broke away and led me into her house.

"This is to remember me," she said. "This is the last time. Just think of it as creating a memory."

She let me make love to her.

In the morning Rose offered me coffee and cinnamon toast with just the right amount of sugar and cinnamon.

"Maybe I should stay," I said.

She just shook her head. "You need to go away and grow up."

"But I love you."

"I know."

"If you're ever dying, tell me, and I will come back."

Rose laughed. "I missed you too, Claude," she said.

I wanted to pretend I couldn't move and lie in her bed all day. I wanted to beg, to say, *I can never live without you*. But I didn't. I got up. I said, "Thank you for breakfast," and I left.

And somehow, even though I am very, very sad, it feels okay. There's a calm inside of me, like the quiet aftermath of a nuclear explosion.

I drive out of town, still picturing my mother on her deathbed. *Where were you when I needed you?* she asks. *I'm sorry*, I say, and she says, *Why didn't you stay? You are all that I have.* I whisper, *I'm sorry. I should have been a better daughter.* She considers this and says, *You weren't such a bad daughter*, and then she dies. I killed her in my fantasy, but somehow that's okay too, part of the calm inside, because I still feel her love. And anyway she is still alive back in Riverton. She will survive without me.

I turn on the radio and the wind is blowing into my car and it's a sunny day and I am driving to San Francisco and I don't know who I'll meet or what I'll do there, and I just had the most mind-blowing bittersweet sex with Rose and I am going away from her and all of it is a giant mess and I'm alive and I'm leaving Riverton. I'm finally fucking leaving town.

# THE HOSPITAL

In the white room nothing will happen. We make the rules in the hospital. We will play roles like doctor and nurse and patient. When we are tired of playing a role, we will switch. There will be no psychiatric hospital scenes. All injuries are physical. All injuries can be healed by the doctor or the surgeon or the nurse or the patient. If the patient does not want the injury cured because they are still attached to it, it will not be cured, or it will heal very slowly. If the patient wants the injury cured immediately, this will be done. Slow healing will be attended to. Nursing will include many layers of bandages, salves, time. Each morning the nurse will look at the wound to see how it is doing. Pleasure will be shown for both fast and slow healing. Sometimes the nurse will smile and hold the hand of the patient and say things like, "You're going to be okay." "You look so much healthier today." "Your leg is really healing." "I love the color of your throat, like a pink rose."

Death does not happen in this hospital. We have nothing against death, but that is another game. If you want to switch to playing death, you must leave this hospital and enter another hospital. Childbirth does not occur in this hospital. If you want to switch to playing childbirth, you must enter another hospital or a birthing pyramid.

I came to the hospital because you are here. You with your hair falling out, you with your quick desire to live like a shot of whiskey going down the throat. You whom I met when you leaned over the bar and whispered, *Fuck me, I'm dying*, and I said, *How do I know you're telling the truth?* and you told me you would show me the test results later, just come to the bathroom with you now, so I followed you and you slid your hands up my skirt and pushed me against the wall and fucked me.

There are three kinds of nurses. One is very attractive and young. She is entirely at home in her body in an unselfconscious way. When she is not being a nurse, she might be skiing or scuba diving. Nurse Two looks like a grandmother. She is very wise. You know she is comfortable with death, which to her is just a door opening. She probably walks through that door sometimes and turns back just to take care of you. Three is the horrible nurse. We cannot leave out the horrible nurse. She is too archetypal. At times, her presence soothes the patient by reminding them of all that is bad in the world—an external pain that can be held against the internal pain and provide comparative relief—but mostly the patients hate the terrible nurse. She is important for their bonding, though. Without the terrible nurse, the patients would not be as close as they are.

Nurse Three hates you and wants to torture you. When she turns you over, it is only to see your bed sores and make a disgusted face. When you ring the bell and she comes, you think she is going to yell at you. Sometimes she does; she says things like "Don't you know we have people who are really sick here?"

In this hospital, you can choose the type of nurse you want. Perhaps you want different nurses at different times.

Today I want the young nurse. She has her limits. She is puppyish in her actions, but I, like so many who are sick, desire to see really healthy flesh. Looking at her gives me a general good feeling. I like the skin at the top of her breasts. It has a slight peach shade to it, and it is firm with tiny white hairs. Her whole body in fact is very much like a peach, even the smell, which is fresh beyond belief. I know that she has many lovers, and this pleases me. I live vicariously through her. Sometimes I catch the scent of the outdoors on her skin, which reminds me of the world beyond the hospital. She is never unhappy. She is always full of vitality.

Of course, you can choose what you are in the hospital for.

I followed you to the hospital. After that night in the bar, I wanted to see you again, but you refused and went away to play the game of being sick, and so I made myself sick to love you.

I am in the hospital for a mysterious disease, which they will never be able to diagnose, though at times I joke with the doctors that perhaps they will name the disease after me. *No,* my extremely handsome doctor with graying temples responds. *They will name it after the doctor who discovers the illness, not the patient.* (I know that he is sleeping with the young nurse, and this pleases me inordinately.) Yes, I understand only famous sports figures get diseases named after them, and yet this mystery disease brings me a great deal of attention. Young doctors often come to examine me and look at my charts. I am proud that I have something so arcane and challenging. My charts are a lovely mishmash of words and graphs and pictures that tell my story. I've always thought there should be a graphic representation of me that I could show people when first meeting them. The charts come in handy for that.

My charts also contain line drawings and x-rays of the food that I eat. I suppose it's childish, but I have them x-ray the food instead of me. There is a complete x-ray record of all the food that I have consumed since I arrived here, because it is something inside the food that's making me sick. I have a theory that we can find this through the x-rays. Some of my x-rayed meals include:

Lamb chop with peas and peach cobbler

Mushroom risotto and crème brûlée

Whole sea bass with passion fruit beurre blanc and wilted greens

Spaghetti (thick as worms) with thin sauce, canned green beans, and apple sauce

Corn dog, Fritos, and Ho Hos

I should mention that the kitchen serves oddly unpredictable fare. So as to seem like any other hospital, they offer traditional, bland food at times, but at other times they have the most wonderful gourmet offerings, cooked by top chefs. Some people prefer the gourmet meals, but the bland ones give us an odd feeling of camaraderie, create an affinity with elementary school children, prisoners, and others who are forced to eat institutional food.

One of the most perplexing aspects of my disease is my becoming sporadically and randomly poisoned by what I eat. Food allergies seem to rise and fall within me. One day I can eat rice and feel fine, but the next week I consume a small amount and it's like I've eaten arsenic. There is vomiting and weakness, and sometimes they have to pump my stomach. If I hadn't had these symptoms before I entered the hospital, I would think perhaps I was being poisoned by the night doctor.

We are all afraid of him. We think perhaps he is a poisoner doctor, like that famous case in England—the doctor who gave elderly women deadly heroin shots. He killed over two hundred people. Why? They say he wanted to be in ultimate control, to decide who lived and who died.

We have a warning system set up. If the night doctor comes into someone's room and offers them an injection, they ring a little bell, and another patient immediately enters. Usually the doctor withdraws when he sees he is being watched. Actually, poisoning is quite common in the medical field. There are nurses who kill their patients. I wonder if there are patients who kill their doctors.

I recently requested a fourth kind of nurse. Everyone was surprised. They felt the three nurse varieties pretty much covered the field. *No,* I said. *These nurses aren't giving me what I need. I want a kind nurse, but an I-don't-take-no-shit-from-anybody nurse. I want a woman from the heartland who has suffered and can look life straight in its shitty eye and still have some warmth in her. I want an I-won't-lie-to-you, you-deserve-the-facts nurse.* Yes, they said. *That kind of a nurse is necessary.* Yes, they said. *Those qualities are in fact the heart of nursing,* and they provided me with Nurse Four.

Really, the relationships I have in the hospital are so much deeper and sweeter than in regular life that I don't want to ever leave. In addition to my rather fond interactions with the nurses, I form strange friendships with other patients. I am especially fond of ones who are dying. They cannot die here, of course, but they can be very near death and still have a wonderful quality to them. They are the funniest people that I know. We laugh about everything.

We could leave at any time if we wanted to, if we decided that our injuries don't really exist or we invented a doctor with cures for them, but we like it here.

You have a kind of disease that makes your skin more and more sensitive. That's why you wanted to fuck at the bar, you say. Now you can only withstand the gentlest touches, and even then you can't take too much. At night, when I sneak into your bed and make love to you so softly that I won't damage any of your organs, I feel more alive than I ever have in my life. You whisper in my ear, *What is it about the closeness of death that makes us so alive?* I whisper back, *I am touching you for the last time. Last time I touch your belly, your mouth. Last time I put your penis in my mouth. Last time, last time.*

# HOSPITAL

After I've been in San Francisco for five months, working temp jobs and learning my way around the city, my mother calls to tell me Hal is in the hospital. He's had a stroke.

I need to see him. I fly back to Riverton with a numbness in my head. I pray, just in case there is a God: *Dear God. Let Hal live. Let him live at least a few more years, and let me see him and tell him I love him.*

I call my temp company and tell them the situation. The woman who hired me, Diana, and I had sex after we met, so she is nice to me and says it's okay. Just call her when I get back in town, and she will find me a new assignment.

Hal was my support when I needed it. In a way, wanting him to live is pure selfishness. I want him to be there for me, if and when I need him. Not that I've called or written him once since I've been gone, but I knew if I asked, he'd help.

When I get back to Riverton, I don't even stop at my mother's house. I drive my rental straight to the hospital. I remember going to this hospital as a child when I needed some stitches. It is a white hospital, and sometimes it's foggy there and you can barely see the outline of the building. That's what I remember about it, that it's like a ghost hospital. You think you see it on the horizon, but maybe it isn't real. Or it exists in between worlds. Maybe it's a ship of a hospital that will sail away with the souls of the dead.

Hospitals are terrifying to me. When I imagine the deaths of people I love, none of them happen in hospitals. It's almost as if the hospital is the worst place to die, because it's the official place to die, and dying should never be official. Dying is personal, and death should never be made to feel like it is sanctioned or allowed or relegated to its own space with paperwork and a form.

Hal's hospital is also very white inside. I guess they make them that way so any dirt sticks out, or maybe to make patients feel nearer to heaven. At the front desk, I ask for Hal. The nurse asks me for a last name, and like an idiot I struggle to remember it.

"Palms," I say. "Hal Palms."

She looks him up in her computer. "Yes, he was checked in four days ago, and he's doing well. He had a stroke, but he's doing pretty well. It was very mild. More of a mini."

Mini-stroke—she makes it sound like marketing jargon. Not ready for a full-sized stroke? What about a mini?

I travel down the most obscenely cold hall. Literally cold. Do they heat this place? The nurses are wearing sweaters. I see a woman being wheeled by, and there is a thick bandage over her head. She looks out of her mind, as if possibly right now her brains are oozing out onto that bandage. What will Hal look like? What is a mini-stroke?

When I find his room, Hal is there looking pretty much like himself, just a little paler.

"Claudia," he says. "My God, it's great to see you. You bring a little life in here. My daughter came with my grandkids, but I pretty much have to toe the official grandfather line with them." He smiles impishly.

He tells me the stroke's not so bad. They caught it right away, and they've just been monitoring him since. There will probably be no permanent physical damage, but he'll need physical therapy on his right leg.

"I won't be able to golf as well," he says.

"I didn't know you played golf."

He is sitting up in bed, and there is a stuffed bunny on the table next to him. Probably something from his family.

"I don't, so it won't be a problem."

I laugh. "That's good."

"I've been here four days, and it's starting to drive me crazy. They should send me home."

I notice flowers around the room, too, and cards. He is loved, but it's still a hospital room that smells of antiseptic and hums with noises from machines.

"I'm glad you're okay," I say. "I was afraid you were going to die."

"Oh, Claudia." He chuckles. "Always the direct one."

Am I direct? "I'm sorry," I say.

"No. I love your honesty. None of my other visitors said it, but it's always the first thing on your mind when someone old gets sick. But no. No death scene here." He smiles and says, "Have a seat. How's San Francisco?"

"I like it," I say, perching on the edge of the bed. "It makes sense there. Being alone feels right there. I mean, I wander around and eat Mexican food a lot, and everyone's a stranger and nobody recognizes me, and that's what I like best. I hang out with Luke on occasion, but he is always chasing men. There are parties. There are a lot of parties, and then there are days when I walk in the street and get lost in the fog. There are also a lot of good bookstores. I have a temp job. It's not so bad. And the ocean. I get to go to the ocean. It's cold and moody and feels like the end of the world."

"Is it exciting?" he says. "Are you on an adventure?"

"I think I am. Whatever was holding me here isn't holding me anymore."

"Good," he says. "You should be an adventurer. I've missed you. Everybody else keeps treating me like I'm old. Not like you, Harold."

"I've missed you too. People keep treating me like I'm young."

He surprises me by reaching up and stroking my face, and I remember our kiss. Except for that one night with Diana, which was fast and sexy and then done, I haven't been touched in a long time. It feels good to be touched by someone who cares for me. Someone who has seen a little of my dark side. I'm not sure how, but I know Hal wants me to touch him too. And I surprise myself with a thought. Sliding off the bed, I go over to the door and shut it. This has been coming for a long time, and it's maybe the wrong thing to do. But maybe it's the right thing. Hal will die someday, and I will too, but we can have this time together. What was it Rose said? Creating a memory.

I take off my blouse. Hal's eyes open wide, but he doesn't say anything—and then he is looking at me like I'm food. Like I'm sustenance. I take off my bra, and he lifts his hands. I step closer so he can run his fingers over and over my breasts. His hands are wrinkled and old, but the fingertips are very soft. He murmurs, "Lovely, lovely."

I return to the hospital door and shove a chair under the handle. I feel strangely aroused. I take my jeans off and drop them at my feet, then I crawl into the hospital bed next to Hal. I pull off my underwear, and he reaches for my pussy, lightly sifting my pubic hair, petting it like an animal, then tracing the outline of my lips, running his finger up and down. His touch is smooth and light, and I want him to push inside of me. I glance at his face to find him watching me, and I feel a kind of calmness in him looking at me, like there is nothing wrong with what we're doing.

"I'm so old," he says. "Why do you even want this?"

Really, I don't know. Why does anyone want anything? We want to feel something. I want to feel him. "I like it," I say.

He pushes his fingers inside me. It feels rough, and yet I am opening easily. He kisses my breast and pushes his hand inside of me. He smells like something from another country, of chemicals and old clothes and scents that he has had on him for a long time.

I reach for his penis, but he says, "No, you don't want to touch an old man's penis."

"It's okay," I say.

"No, Claudia. I just want to touch you like this. Give you pleasure."

He keeps moving his hand, and I rock back and forth on his fingers as his thumb rubs my clit. When I come, I cry, and it feels like a knife in my heart. I miss Rose.

When I relax in his arms, he starts to cry too. "I miss my wife so much," he says. "When you're old, everyone dies around you, and you can either break down and break down or become hard and lose part of yourself. I thought no one would ever let me touch them like this again." He hugs me to his body. "Always let someone touch you," he says, "even if you don't love them. Touching is as important as love."

He holds me in his arms like a lover and a child, crying, his face contorted and ugly, and I can see just how old he is, and how he has long hairs growing out of his ears and his skin is getting bald in one spot and his earlobes are empty, wrinkled sacks and he still looks lovely to me. Not lovely like I'm in love with him, just lovely like another person can be.

I hear a ringing bell somewhere in the hospital and become aware again of the cool disinfectant smell in the room. On the floor is someone's arm band, which is really strange, and there are some Kleenex next to the bed, and on the silver cart is some food Hal didn't finish—peaches in light syrup and a chicken patty sandwich and an energy bar. I grab the energy bar and eat half of it, but I still feel weak, like maybe I am dying. This is it. We do this. We live for a second, and then we die, and everything that ever happened becomes lost and decomposes.

I lie on Hal's chest for a while. He falls asleep. I feel oddly safe here in the terrifying hospital. Soon I'll get up and go visit my mother and then fly back to San Francisco and keep looking for a better job and a lover and whatever I need to do to become myself, but right now I can rest—and I have even given someone something for a change. I gave Hal a little bit of life, a little bit of being young. I'm not as ancient as I sometimes feel. I'm twenty-four years old. Maybe it's wrong to give sex like a gift, but maybe it isn't. Hal is making a slight wheezing noise when he breathes in. He smells like an old man, like medicine and Vicks VapoRub. He smells a little like death, and now so do I.

# DREAM

On the third day back in San Francisco, I wake up sweaty from a dream. The sheets are around my ankles, like I've been fighting them.

I remember looking into Rose's eyes in the dream, and she looked into mine. I need to tell her.

It's 5:00 a.m. here, but 8:00 there. Thank God for time zones. Luke and my housemates are asleep. I trudge down the long hallway to the kitchen. The phone is in a nook next to the kitchen. I lie down on the old love seat with the red velvet cover, where usually I go to read a book and watch my roommates cook a stir fry or drink coffee. I dial, which takes a minute. We have an old yellow rotary phone. Rose's phone rings and rings, and her answering machine switches on: "Hey, this is Rose. I'd love to hear what you have to say."

"Rose," I say. "I need to tell you this dream I had. I don't know why. I just do. In the dream I was in the bathroom. I was pregnant, and someone put me in the bathtub, a clawfoot tub like we have here. I realized the man was Hal. I looked down, and all the water was red. Someone called it *bloody show*. I felt these strong pains, and I realized I was in labor and had to get to the hospital. Actually, there was someone else there, a woman. Then I realized it was you. I said, 'I can't believe I don't have a hospital picked. Help me!' You looked into my eyes, and said, 'We'll go to the Harrisburg hospital.' Then we start walking to the hospital where I was born. I don't know why we were walking, Rose. It doesn't seem at all practical."

The answering machine cuts off with a couple of beeps.

I call again. It rings again, and rings. "Hey, this is Rose. I'd love to hear what you have to say."

I like hearing her voice, even though it's not her. I'm afraid of waking my housemates—I know the masseuse came home around 3:00 a.m. from a rave—so I whisper.

"Hal and you and I were walking a long way to the hospital. After a while I felt like the baby was starting to be born. We were near the hospital, but it was coming out of me. I thought, *Oh my God, the baby is half born*. I knew not to push. I was trying to hold it, but then I reached down and felt part of its head out, and I thought, *I need to just have this baby, because if this much is out and it can't breathe, it'll suffocate*. The baby comes out of me. It's not breathing. I think, *Oh, fuck, is this baby going to be dead? Did I just give birth to a stillborn baby?*"

The machine cuts off again.

I call back. My fingers are getting tired from dialing. It rings only once.

"Did the baby live?" Rose asks.

"Hi, I thought you weren't answering. It's good to hear *you* you."

"I was listening. Did the baby live?"

"At first it was blue and looked dead. It had a lot of goo on its face. It was under a caul, almost like a mummy. I brushed some of the stuff off and breathed into its mouth. I knew to do that, but I'd never done it before. I wasn't sure it would work. But the baby started breathing. I was worried about stopping, so I breathed into its mouth a little more, and he was definitely alive!"

"I'm glad the baby lived," she says.

"Me too. I felt such joy, Rose. I still feel it now. And you were the one who led me to the hospital. You definitely helped it be born."

"But you never made it to the hospital. You gave birth on your own like some Alaskan homesteader."

"That's true," I say with an odd sense of pride. "I was pretty damn self-sufficient."

"You are so strange, calling and telling me your dreams."

"I know, but I had to because you were part of the dream. I mean, maybe you were the father. It was unclear."

"I don't know how dream conception works, but I'm sure it's much more lesbian-friendly than the real kind."

She pauses, and I hear her breathing.

"You're in my dreams too, Claude."

"Thanks for picking up," I say, my eyes prickling.

I hear someone getting up in the house, then Luke is trudging down the hallway, half asleep, to the bathroom.

"You doing okay?" Rose asks.

"Yeah, I saved the baby." I whisper so Luke doesn't hear.

"Yes, you certainly did. I have to get ready for work. Bye, Claude," she says and hangs up.

I sneak back to my room. Luke will be mad if he finds out about the call. He says I should leave Rose alone, for her sake and mine. He's right, but God it felt good to talk to her. And that baby. I think about its mouth again, how filled with goo and fluids it was, how I swept that away with my fingers and then breathed into its small, small mouth until it was breathing too.

## DEAR POTENTIAL LOVER,

I know you can't understand all of this, my notes to you, my fantasies, my ramblings. How could you when even I can't understand it all? Still, maybe I will tuck these notes into some libraries here and there, hoping that they might get to you. That you'll find my book at exactly the right time. And maybe I will find you—in San Francisco, on the BART—and you'll be wearing mismatched socks, and I will love you for that. Because to take the time to match socks is to throw away months of your life. You might be old or young, or a woman or a man—I don't really know— but you will be reading a book about obscure sexual practices of some obscure tribe, and I will know it's you because you'll miss your stop, so caught up in what it might be like to display your mineral-reddened genitals to strangers. And I will sit next to you, so out of the corner of your eye you see the edge of my thigh, and I will say, quietly, so only you can hear, "I'm willing to be an anthropologist with you." You, thinking I'm crazy, will get up and move, but you will think about my offer afterward and realize that you blew a brilliant opportunity for field research. Every day after that you will look for me on the train, and maybe someday our paths will cross again, and you will have the perfect line all ready in your mouth. You will lean across the train and say, softly, so no one else can hear: "I'll be your informant."

# Acknowledgments

So many people to thank.

Thank you to Michelle Boisseau and James Baker Hall for being amazing teachers.

To Nicola Mason and Acre Books for believing in the book and making it better, and to Barbara Neely Bourgoyne for creating a cover of wonder and passion that tells the whole story in one glance.

To my many readers who gave me feedback, support and encouragement: Ariana Souzis, Olga Zilberbourg, Rachel Chalmers, Celeste Chan, Sonya Worthy, Liz Worthy, Chaim Bertman, Adam Tobin, Camille Roy, Mary Berger, Michele Mortimer, Jan Richman, and Cara Stimpson.

To Sasha Cagen for being my always and eternal writing buddy, editor, and friend.

To Josh Wilson and *The Fabulist* and Roxane Gay and *PANK* for publishing some chapters as short stories. To Kate Schatz for publishing an article about an early version of this book in *Kitchen Sink*. To *Anything That Moves* magazine for support and bisexual visibility. And to my wonderful community at the Writers Grotto for showing me how writers do it!

To my dear friends Wendy Repass, Brett Litton, Carla Harting, Bernie Kellman, Russell Gonzaga, and Mary Crockett Hill for always being there. To my sister Beth Maurer for loving me through my difficult years (are they over?).

And to Adam, Al, Gerry, and Kai Souzis for all your support and love.

This book took a long time to finish and even longer to get published, so if you are a writer in that situation and feel like your book might never be born, keep going—persistence isn't just a dirty word.